MILENA BUSQUETS

Milena Busquets was born in Barcelona where she attended the Lycée Français de Barcelone. She obtained a degree in archaeology from the Institute of Archaeology at University College London, began work in publishing, and has since founded her own publishing house. She currently works as a journalist and as a translator.

MILENA BUSQUETS

This Too Shall Pass

Translated from the Spanish
by Valerie Miles

VINTAGE

1 3 5 7 9 10 8 6 4 2

Vintage
20 Vauxhall Bridge Road,
London SW1V 2SA

Vintage is part of the Penguin Random House group of companies
whose addresses can be found at global.penguinrandomhouse.com

Penguin
Random House
UK

First published in Vintage in 2017
First published in trade paperback by Harvill Secker in 2016

First published with the title *También esto pasará* in Spain
by Anagrama in 2015

www.vintage-books.co.uk

A CIP catalogue record for this book is
available from the British Library

ISBN 9781784701628

This book has been selected to receive financial assistance from
English PEN's "Pen Translates!" programme, supported by Arts
Council England. English PEN exists to promote literature and our
understanding of it, to uphold writers' freedoms around the world,
to campaign against the persecution and imprisonment of writers for
stating their views, and to promote the friendly co-operation of
writers and the free exchange of ideas. www.englishpen.org

Typeset by Palimpsest Book Production Ltd, Falkirk, Stirlingshire
Printed and bound by Clays Ltd, St Ives Plc

Penguin Random House is committed to a sustainable future
for our business, our readers and our planet. This book is made
from Forest Stewardship Council® certified paper.

For Noé and Héctor. And for Esteban and Esther.

1

For some strange reason, I never considered what it would be like to be forty. When I was twenty, I could imagine myself at thirty, living with the love of my life and a bunch of kids. Or at sixty, baking apple pies with my grandchildren – me who can't boil an egg to save my soul, but I would learn. Even at eighty, as an old bag drinking whisky with my girlfriends. But I never imagined myself at forty, not at fifty either. And yet here I am. It's my mother's funeral, and if that's not bad enough, I'm forty. I have no idea how I got here, how I got to this town that suddenly makes me want to puke. I swear I've never dressed so badly in my entire life. When I get home I'm going to burn every last stitch of clothing I have on today – they're all drenched in exhaustion and sadness, there's nothing worth saving. All my friends are here today, and a few of hers, and some others who don't seem to be friends of anybody. A huge crowd of people, and yet some of the important ones are missing. Illness evicted her from her throne so cruelly in the end, it completely destroyed her kingdom, and pretty much screwed us all up one way or another. And you pay for those things when the funeral comes round. First there's you, Mum, the dead person, who fucked them over, and then me, the daughter, whom they were never fond of anyway. It's all your fault, Mum, you know that? Little by little, unawares, the weight of your dwindling happiness found its place on my shoulders. And it weighed so heavily, so heavily, even when I was far away, even when I began to understand and accepted what was happening, even when I separated myself from you for a while, because I realised that if I didn't, you wouldn't be the only casualty left in the wreckage. But I do think you loved me, not a lot, not a little, you just loved me, full stop. I have always thought that people who say 'I love you so much', actually love you very little, or maybe they add the 'so much', which in this case really means 'so little', out of awkwardness, or fear at the sheer command of an 'I love you', which is the only real way of saying 'I love you'. The 'so much' turns it into some-thing for the general public, when it's never meant to be. 'I love you', the magic words that can turn you into a dog, or a god, a lunatic, a shadow. Anyway, most of your friends were 'progressive', though I don't think that's what they call them now, or maybe they don't even exist as a collective any more. They didn't believe in God, or life after death. I remember when it was so fashionable not to believe in God. Nowadays, people gawp at you in embarrassment if you say you don't believe in God, or in Vishnu, or Mother Earth, or reincarnation, or the spirit of something or other, or in anything at all, and they say: 'Oh, so you're not illuminated.' The people who didn't show up to the funeral must have calculated the situation and decided: 'Better to stay home, on the couch, with a bottle of wine, and pay respects in my own way, which will be more meaningful than going to the mountains with her idiot offspring. After all, funerals are just another social convention.' Or something like that. Because I imagine they forgave you, if there was anything to forgive, and that they loved you.

As a young girl, I used to watch you all laugh together, playing cards until the sun came up, roving and skinny-dipping and going out for dinner, and I think you had fun, you were happy. The problem with families of choice is that they disappear more easily than the blood ones. The adults I grew up with are either dead or living who knows where. They're certainly not here, under the blazing sun that's melting my skin and cracking the earth. I know this narrow, winding trail through the olive grove by heart. Despite only spending a few months a year in the town, it is, or was, the way home, leading to all the things we liked. I don't know where it leads now. I should have grabbed a hat to wear, although it'd just be another thing to throw away. I feel dizzy. I think I'm going to sit down next to this dreadful angel with swords for wings and never get up again. And here's Carolina, always so aware of everything; she takes me by the arm and leads me over to the wall where nobody can see us. From here I can catch sight of the sea, now close by, just beyond a hill of exhausted olive trees. Mum, you promised that when you died my life would be on track and structured, that the pain would be bearable. You never said I would feel like ripping my guts out and eating them. And you told me these things before you started lying. There was a moment when you, a person who never told a fib, started lying and I don't know what sparked it. The friends who have gone out of their way to be here weren't around you much towards the end, they remember the glorious person you were ten or ten thousand years ago. And here are my friends, Carolina, Mercè, Elisa and Sofía. Mum, in the end we decided not to bury Patum with you. This isn't Pharaoh's Egypt, you know. I appreciate how convinced you were that her life would have no meaning without you, but if you stop to think about it, she's a big dog and she would never have fitted in the niche – I can just imagine the two undertakers pushing her in the bum to squish her in, like we used to do so many times at sea, to get her up the steps and onto the boat after a swim – and, anyway, I'm pretty sure the whole idea of being buried with a dog, well, it's illegal. Even if she were dead, like you. Because you are dead, Mum. I've been saying that over and over for two days now, asking my friends again and again in case it's just some big mistake or maybe a misunderstanding, but they've assured me every time that the unthinkable has happened. Aside from the fathers of my children, there is only one interesting man here, and he's a stranger. I know, here I am on the verge of collapsing from the horror and the heat, and despite everything, my radar can still hone right in on the presence of an attractive man. It must be the survival instinct kicking in. I ask myself what are the protocols of hooking up with someone in a cemetery. I ask myself whether he'll come up to me to pay his respects. I don't think so. Coward. A handsome coward though – but what is a coward doing at my mother's funeral, the least cowardly person I've ever known in my entire life? Maybe that girl by your side, holding your hand and staring at me so adamantly and with such curiosity, is your girlfriend. Isn't she a little short for you? OK, midget girlfriend of the mysterious coward, today is my mother's funeral, I have the right to do and say whatever I want. As if it was my birthday. Can't hold it against me.

The funeral is almost over. Twenty minutes in all, the silence nearly complete, no speeches, no poems – you promised you'd rise from the dead and haunt us for eternity if we let any of your poet friends recite – no prayers, no flowers, no music. It would've been even shorter if the geriatric undertakers who were charged with hoisting the coffin into the niche hadn't been so clumsy. I get that the beautiful man is not going to approach me and change my life, though I can't think of a better and more suitable time than this; however, he could have had the decency to help the pair of fossils when the coffin almost fell to the ground. One of them shouted, 'Bloody hell!' These are the only words pronounced at the funeral. They seem very appropriate ones, very precise. I guess all funerals I attend from now on will be yours. We take off slowly down the hill. Carolina grabs my hand. It's over. My mother is dead. I think I'll head over to the municipal register in Cadaqués. Now that you live here, it's the best place for me, too.

2

To the best of my knowledge, the only thing that moment-
arily alleviates the sting of death – and life – without
leaving a hangover is sex. It only lasts a few seconds,
though; maybe a little longer if you fall asleep afterwards.
But then the furniture, the clothes, the memories, the
lamps, the panic, the grief, everything that had been
whooshed up into the *The Wizard of Oz* tornado comes
right back down and falls into its place in the room, in
the head, in the belly. I open my eyes and it's not garlands
of flowers and singing dwarfs that I see, no; I'm lying in
bed next to my ex. The house is quiet except for the cries
of children playing in the swimming pool outside, drifting
in through the open window. The clear blue light brings
the promise of yet another day of sun and heat, and I
watch the tops of the sycamore trees sway serenely from
my bed, remarkably indifferent to misfortune. Apparently,
there was no event of spontaneous combustion in the
deep of the night, the branches haven't turned into

murderous, flying swords, no blood is dripping from them – nothing like that has occurred. I look at Oscar out of the corner of my eye without daring to move, aware that my slightest gesture could awaken him; it's been a while since we slept together. I take in his long, firm body and slightly concave chest, his narrow hips and cyclist's legs, his large, unequivocally masculine features, somewhat animal-like in their expressiveness and robustness. 'I like that he has a man's face,' my mother told me after running in to him for the first time in the lift of our building and realising, without needing an introduction, that this bull-headed boy with his shy teenage body, always hunched forward just a little, was on his way to my apartment. And she said flirtingly: 'It's so hot that I can have a shower fully dressed, sit down to write with my clothes soaking wet, and within half an hour they're already dry!' By the time he got to my apartment he was roaring with laughter. 'I think I just met your mother,' he said as I quivered with impatience. Oscar's body was my only home for a while, my only place in the world. Then we had a son. And finally we got to know each other. One tries to behave as a forest creature, guided by instinct, by one's skin, the cycles of the moon, responding promptly and gratefully and with a little relief, to the calling of all that doesn't require thought, that's already been measured and decided for you by your body or the stars. Yet there always comes the day when it's time to stand up and start talking. What theoretically has happened just once in our collective history, when humans went from scuttling around on four legs to standing straight and using reason, is what happens to me every time I fall out of love. And every time, it's a crash-landing. I've lost count of how often we've tried to get back together. Something always gets in the way, usually it has to do with his strong character, or mine. He has a girlfriend now, but that hasn't stopped us from sharing a bed today, or from his being by my side over these six dark months of hospitals and doctors and battles that were lost before they'd even begun. Mum, what got into you? How did you ever think you could win this battle, the last one, the one nobody ever wins? Not the smartest, nor the strongest, not the bravest or the most generous, not even the ones who deserve it the most. I could have reconciled with a peaceful death. We had discussed death so many times, but we never thought the bitch would take your head before taking the rest, that she would leave you with a few little crumbs of intermittent lucidity, just enough to make you suffer a little bit more.

Oscar is a firm believer in the healing power of sex, the sort of man whose natural pluck and robust condition lead him to the idea that there is nothing whatsoever, no disgrace, no disturbance, no disappointment, that a little sex can't fix. Feeling sad? Fuck. Have a headache? Fuck. Computer crashed? Fuck. You're broke? Fuck. Your mother died? Fuck. Sometimes it works. I slink out of bed. Oscar is also of the mind that making love is the best way to start the day off. I prefer to be invisible in the morning, and don't reach my full mind–body union until around lunchtime.

The sink is brimming with dirty plates, and the fridge offers a meagre pair of expired yogurts, a wrinkly apple and a couple of beers. I open one, since there's no coffee or tea left. The trees waggle their leaves outside the living-room window to bid me good morning, and I see that the blinds are down at the elderly woman's place opposite ours, so she must already be on holiday, or maybe she died, it's hard to say. It feels as though I've been living in some other place for months. I'm still covered in last night's sweat, mixed with a little of the bull man's, too. I sniff below the collar of my shirt and distinguish a foreign smell, the invisible traces left by the blissful invasion of my body by another one, of my skin – so compliant and permeable – by someone else's skin, of my sweat by someone else's sweat. Sometimes not even a shower can erase the hint of it, which I notice for days, like a lewd but flattering dress that grows ever fainter, until it disappears altogether. I touch my temple with the bottle of beer and close my eyes. This is supposedly my favourite time of the year, but now I have no plans. Your decline has been the only plan on my calendar for months, maybe years. I hear Oscar tinkering around in the bedroom. He calls out to me.

— Come here, quick, I have something important to tell you.

It's one of his sexual ploys and I pretend not to hear him. If I pay attention, we won't get back out of bed until lunch, and I don't have time for that; death carries with it a thousand administrative details. He continues griping and calling out to me for ten solid minutes. He says he can't find his pants, I must have hidden them – sure, I have nothing better to do right now than play hide-and-seek with your underwear. He finally comes out of my bedroom, doesn't say a word, just walks up behind me and starts kissing my neck, pressing me up against the table. I continue organising my papers as if nothing's going on. He nips hard at my ear. I cry out. I don't know whether to smack him or not. By the time I make up my mind and raise my hand, it's already too late. You can tell a lot about a man by the way he takes off your knickers and flicks them aside. And the animal in me – perhaps the only thing that hasn't been reduced to ashes over the past few months – arches her back, grabs the table for support and tenses her entire body. Just as I'm about to haul off and give him that smack, my other heart begins to throb, the one just invaded by his cock, and once that happens, nothing else matters.

— You shouldn't drink beer in the morning, Blanquita. Or smoke, he adds, watching me light a cigarette.

He looks at me with the same mixture of pity and concern as everyone else over the past few days, and I'm not sure whether these expressions are a reflection of what's on my face, or vice versa. I haven't really looked in the mirror for a long time, or have glanced without really seeing myself, just to straighten up a little. This specular relationship has never been under so much strain. My mirror, *mon semblable, mon frère*, wishes to remind me that the party is over. But there's tenderness in the way Oscar's looking at me too, which is a feeling akin to love, it's not just pity and concern. I'm not accustomed to being the object of people's sympathy and it makes my stomach heave. Would you please just go back to looking at me the way you did five minutes ago? Just turn me back into an object, a toy? Something to possess and that gives you pleasure, not full of despair, not somebody who just lost the person she loved the most in life and who sped through the streets of Barcelona on a motorcycle, but still didn't get there in time?

— I think you should take off for a few days, get some fresh air. There's nothing for you to do here and the city's completely deserted.

— Yeah, you're right.

— I don't want you to be by yourself.

— No.

I don't mention that I'd been feeling alone for months now.

— The worst is over.

I burst out laughing.

— The worst and the best. Everything is over.

— There are a lot of people who care about you.

I don't know how many times I've heard this over the past few days. The silent, chatty army of people who care about me has risen up at the precise moment when all I want is to go to bed and be left alone. With my mother by my side, holding my hand and brushing my forehead with hers.

— Yeah, yeah, I know. Much obliged. I don't tell him that I don't believe in other people's love – even my mother stopped loving me for a while – because love is the most unreliable thing in the world.

— Why don't you spend a few days in Cadaqués? It's your house now.

How can you say that, you stupid, foolish, disrespectful brute? I think in a snap as I look him right in those big, caring, concerned eyes. It's my mother's house. And it always will be.

— I don't know, I respond.

— The boat's already in the water. It'll do you good to be there.

Maybe you're right, I tell myself. The town witches have always protected me. Cadaqués is a remote place, isolated by mountains and only accessible by way of a hellish road, where savage winds drive anyone who doesn't strictly deserve the beauty of its skies, the pinkish light of its summer sunsets, completely mad. I've seen the witches there since I was a little girl, scrambling over the bell tower, cackling or scowling, expelling or embracing the newly arrived, instigating arguments between lovesick couples, instructing the jellyfish as to which legs or bellies to sting, placing sea urchins strategically just below the right feet. I've seen how they'd paint breathtaking sunrises to alleviate the most apalling hangovers, turn each of the town's streets and hidden corners into welcoming bedrooms, blanket you in velvety waves that wash the cares and troubles of the world away. And, well, there's a new witch now.

— Yeah, maybe you're right. Cadaqués. I'm going to Cadaqués. And I add: — Tara! Home. The red earth of Tara, I'll go home to Tara . . . After all, tomorrow is another day.

I take a long pull of my beer.

— What film is that from? I ask him.

I think you're mixing *Gone with the Wind* and *E.T.*, he says chuckling.

— Oh, yeah, you're right. The beer on an empty stomach is making me say really idiotic things. — How many times did I force you to watch *Gone with the Wind*?

— Many times.

— And how many times did you fall asleep?

— Nearly every one.

— Yeah, you've always had crappy taste in films. You're such a snob.

For once he doesn't talk back, he just looks at me with a smile on his face, eyes full of wishful thinking. Oscar is one of the few adult men I know whose face can express the eagerness of hope, as if he were expecting the Three Kings. I've never told him this; I'd prefer he didn't know. Hope is the hardest facial expression to fake and the ability to express it diminishes with every broken dream; the only thing that can substitute the loss is ordinary desire.

— It'll be OK, Blanca, you'll see.

— I know, I lie.

He has to go to Paris for a few days for work, he says, but as soon as he gets back he'll come up to Cadaqués. He sighs and adds: — I'm not sure what to do with my girlfriend. Men always, always, always have to screw things up. My face takes on the air of deep concern, another expression that's tough to fake, though not as much as hope, and I slam the door.

Don't know what I'm going to do without my mother.

3

Nicolas thinks you're up in heaven playing poker with Snowflake (Barcelona Zoo's late albino gorilla). Despite only being five years old, he's so staunchly convinced that it's true, he sometimes makes me wonder. From the height of my forty years, I may have known you infinitely more closely, but in the latter days I think the children were the only ones able to work the miracle of accessing you, seeing through the haze of illness to face the person you had been. They alone were truly caring and clever enough to resuscitate you. They are the lucky ones, they never hated you for a minute – I can't imagine a better place for you. Now he draws you in his pictures flying over our heads, a blend of teasing witch and awkward fairy godmother, not very different from the way you were in real life.

They just got back from spending a few days with Guillem, the father of my elder son. They're suntanned, a little taller and salad-laden, with tomatoes and cucumbers

fresh from Guillem's garden. I always accept these offer-
ings of fruits and vegetables with a show of enthusiasm
and end up throwing them all in the bin with the first
insect that rears its ugly head when I'm cleaning them,
especially given my scant interest in all things agrarian.

— Guillem, the only apples for me are the kind Snow
White eats. I don't like eco apples because every time I
go to take a bite, I feel like I'm about to decapitate a
worm. It makes me queasy. Get it?

— Sure, so you prefer poisoned apples, huh? Well, never
fear, we'll bring a few next time – they might just do the
trick.

He acts out the gesture of cutting his throat, with his
eyes closed and tongue lolling, sending the children into
a fit of giggles. They adore his mixture of silliness and
common sense, how he can bring the events of the French
Revolution to life, and then run out to the garden and
plant tomatoes.

Guillem is an archaeologist, a drinker, he's cultivated,
caring and intelligent, a Catalan through and through,
considerate, a cheat, strong, cagey, generous, a lot of fun
and very stubborn. His motto is 'I'm not in the mood
for kicking up shit' and except for the years when we were
together, when his mood seemed perfect for kicking up
a lot of shit, he pretty much adheres to it. We have a
love–hate relationship. I love him and he pretends to hate
me all the time. But his hatred brings more good things
than the love of most of the people I've known. He kept

Patum, my mother's dog, since she'd been ours for a few years before we separated. We left her in my mother's care once to go on a trip, and when I went to pick her up, she told me she was keeping her, that Patum would be better off with her mother and sister. So you kept our dog, Mum. You made her yours, like you did with everything you loved, with everyone, you took their lives away from them, and gave each one another life back, much larger and more carefree and fun than anything they'd known before or after. But it came with a price, it meant living under your relentless scrutiny, like prisoners of a love that as you yourself described would never, ever, in a million years, be blind. Except for the dogs, maybe, but only them. Patum outlived her mother and her sister. I knew the end was approaching the day you let us take her back and there was no argument about how she couldn't stay with you any more. If you were willing to let your dog go, you were willing to let everything go. We'd been in a free fall for two years, and the bottom of the precipice was nigh. That afternoon, with your hand still within my reach, I initiated the process to have you buried at the cemetery in Port Lligat. Patum came to your funeral, the only dog there. Guillem dressed her collar with a black ribbon – the kind of idea that would occur to him – and she behaved like a perfect lady. She didn't sprawl with her legs out everywhere like she usually does, but sat up solemnly and primly in the shade sporting her black ribbon. Guillem wore his old jeans and a shirt, ironed especially for the occasion, that pulled just a little bit at the belly. I think you would have liked the image of it, you would have sat down next to them – not much in the mood for kicking up shit either – your hand patting your dog's head, observing the silent funeral. Who knows, you might even have been there.

— Well, Blanquita, as you can see the children have been fed well. Right, guys?

They both agree, well instructed.

— No frozen pizzas, none of those nasty toxic noodles your mother likes to feed you?

They both say no.

— Yeah, Mum, we ate really well, Nicolas, the younger one, says.

— I'm so glad to hear that.

— By the way, you know they've banned those pre-cooked noodles you're so fond of, don't you? Guillem says. Now you'll have to buy them on the black market.

He laughs. I glare at him with hatred in my eyes until a giggle escapes.

— And they've been to the swimming pool every day. Every day. When was the last time you took them to the pool?

— Never, the two boys exclaim in unison.

Guillem smiles triumphantly.

— Mum, they sell cheese puffs at the pool Guillem takes us to. And they make him special gin and tonics.

Guillem signals with his hand for them to keep quiet.

— Gin and tonics, huh? Who wouldn't want to go to a pool like that?! And cheese puffs. They're grown ecologically too?

— All righty then . . . No, seriously, it's good for the children to spend time outdoors, in the fresh air, and there's nothing for them to do here. This city is unbearable in the summer. Actually, it's unbearable all year round. Why don't you go up to Cadaqués for a few days? You'll enjoy it there. The boat's in the water, isn't it?

Yes, *Tururut* is in the water. My mother took care of everything.

You know, Mum, how crazy was that? Did you really think you'd be able to go boating? I wonder if the sea is there now, without you. Is it the same sea? Or will it have turned in on itself and become a tiny thing, like a neatly folded napkin that you carried off with you in your pocket?

— That settles it then – I'm sure she would have wanted us to take advantage of it.

I accompany Guillem to the door; he pats me on the shoulder a few times.

— Come on, cheer up. We'll hang out in Cadaqués next week, OK? You'll see – it'll be great. Peaceful.

4

One of the best ways to discover your home town's secret hiding places – and I don't mean those little romantic spots, but more like the truly unlikely ones – is by falling in love with a married man. That's the only way to explain how I got to be in Badalona, I think it's Badalona, eating truly disgusting croquettes that taste so perfectly delicious to us, in a filthy two-bit bar that seems like the most delightful place on earth, promising to return soon, as eager and worldly as if we were at the Ritz. I hadn't seen Santi in weeks. Since before you died. Those months while you struggled uselessly and brutally against the disease and dementia, I, when I wasn't too sad or tired, struggled in the same place, equally uselessly and at times brutally, to prove to myself, to prove to the world, that I was still alive. The opposite of death is life, is sex. And as the disease encroached and grew more fierce and unrelenting, so my sexual relationships also grew more fierce and unrelenting, as if upon every bed on the face of the earth there was a single battle being waged: yours. The desperate fuck desperately, it's a known fact. So farewell to the mornings when I opened my eyes, alone or in someone's arms, and thought, 'happy': the world is a little smaller than my bedroom. Sometimes it felt as though we were both turning into dry, brittle trees, grey as ghosts about to turn to dust. But when I told you as much, you assured me it wasn't so, that we were the two strongest people you'd ever known, and that no storm would ever get the better of us.

Santi's wearing my favourite jeans, they're totally worn out in faded red tones, and a khaki-coloured parka we bought together a long time ago. I think he put them on to seduce me, but also as an amulet against the storms that often afflict our relationship. When I see him coming for me straight as an arrow, dodging cars while standing up on his bike pedals as if he were twenty years old instead of twice that age, with those torn red jeans and that tight brown body, my pulse quickens. His body is more toned from the waist down than the waist up from so much skiing and cycling, and his worker's hands, short-fingered and fleshy, are often marked with cuts or bruises, and he always makes my heart skip a beat. I think that's why I keep going back: he takes my breath away every time. You always used to tell me with mock concern: 'Your problem is that you like good-looking men.' But I think deep down this one childish, masculine trait of mine always amused you, of preferring something as free, as random and pointless as a pleasing appearance to power, intelligence or money.

We have a few beers and decide to catch a quick bite; we haven't seen each other for a long time, and we're both so anxious to be together, it's hard to keep our hands to ourselves. I brush his waist, he touches my shoulder, caresses my little finger when he lights my cigarette, we stand about five centimetres too close for what is proper between a couple of friends. We stroll down the narrow streets looking for a quiet, solitary place away from the sun, and when we find a subterranean passageway, he pushes me up against the wall, kisses me and plunges his hand down my trousers. The only reason men's physical strength should exist is to give us pleasure, to squeeze away every last drop of sorrow or fear left inside. A teenager with a backpack saunters by looking at us sideways, trying to pretend he hasn't noticed as he picks up his stride a little. I've almost forgotten those tangled first kisses, the eagerness and bruises of the awkward times that came before I learned the value of slowness and immobility, the precise movements of a surgeon, when one goes from only fucking with the body to also fucking with the head.

— They're going to arrest us for public indecency, I whisper in his ear.

He laughs, and wrests himself a few excruciating centimetres away from me, gently smoothing my trousers and shirt back to their proper places as if I were a little girl, the same way as when he helps his daughters get dressed.

— We could come back and fuck here some night. Don't you think? I say. — Like a couple of teenagers.

— Sure we can.

— I'll wear a skirt, it'll make it easier.

He grabs me by the hand.

— Why don't we get something to eat first, Jezebel?

— There's nothing like vertical love. Everyone knows that, I say.

And he gives me a fucking kick in my bum.

And there's the ice cube melting woefully in my glass of white wine. The waiter had placed it decisively and without consultation, when I told him that just maybe the wine wasn't sufficiently chilled. Santi is chit-chatting chirpily with the owner of the bar and pinching my knee. A man who isn't kind to the waiters, I tell myself, is not kind to anyone, and will end up not being kind to you either. I congratulate him effusively for his wild-mushroom croquettes, which are unquestionably of the frozen variety. He looks at my cleavage and smiles.

— Have I ever told you my theory about why some men are so obsessed with food? I ask him. — I think it's because they don't fuck enough. All the city's posh restaurants stay in business thanks to them. Haven't you ever noticed how they're always chock-full of middle-aged couples? Men sporting watches as expensive as cars, busy talking about croquette recipes, and women who look off into infinity with irked, pinched faces counting their calories.

— And have I ever told you my theory that when you want to fuck around, it's because you want to fuck around?

— It's never occurred to me, no. Could be.

He grabs me around the ribcage with both hands like a human corset and squeezes until his fingers almost touch.

— How can you have such big tits with such a small frame?

— My friend Sofía thinks that big breasts are a hassle and says they should be like dicks: they grow when you need them and then just stay nice and reasonably sized when you don't. Retracting tits.

He laughs. — Your friends are nuts. So are you.

He asks the waiter to pour two more drinks. I feel as though I've drunk a lot already. There's almost no more wine left in the bottle and I'm pretty sure it was almost full when we got here. Santi kisses me holding my face in his two hands, as if I were going to escape. He asks for more croquettes, which I don't touch, and says to the waiter sighing and looking concerned: — She won't eat for me.

— Eat, lady, eat.

I nibble half of a croquette and wash it down briskly.

— Let's make a toast, he says, — to us.

— To us.

We stay quiet for a moment, staring at each other.

— My life's a piece of shit. I'm a total mess, he murmurs suddenly.

— Me too, I answer.

I let out a bark, or what Guillem calls my hyena's cackle, which he taught the children to imitate perfectly, or what my psychiatrist calls my anxious laugh.

— How's work?

— The partners haven't been paid for three months. Not a single architectural firm in this country has work now, there's not a single building under construction. We have no idea what's going to happen.

— What a disaster.

— As of right now, even if I wanted to, I would never be able to get a separation – I wouldn't be able to pay the rent.

Another example of the inevitable triumph in the struggle for gender equality, where it seems as though men have become more like us, instead of the other way round. Now men can't get divorced either, or they'll lose their social standing, I think not without a pang of melancholy.

— And I wouldn't be able to go skiing, he adds candidly.

— Yeah, well, wouldn't that be the tragedy?

— Don't be such a bitch!

I've been seeing Santi for nearly two years. I've never wanted to be privy to the details of his relationship with his wife, out of tact, respect and apprehension. Generally speaking, I think it's far better to know as little as possible about people. Though it's really only a question of time, a little, and keeping your eyes and ears open, before sooner or later their true self comes out.

— I would have liked to be there with you at the funeral.

— Shall we? I say, standing up.

We locate a nice little hotel, somewhat old-fashioned and family-friendly, right on the beachfront.

— Is it OK? You like it?

— Yeah, it's fine.

He asks for a room with a view for naptime, and I start unbuttoning my blouse. The receptionist looks at us undaunted, and continues typing away at her computer. We ask for a gin and tonic while we wait for the room to be readied and go outside. The beach is nearly empty, only a few bodies scattered around here and there, looking vulgar, made ugly by the stark noonday sun, the lack of privacy and promiscuity. Even the most uncomfortable, sick and shattered body can be grandiose and captivating, but a hundred bodies lying next to each other under the sun never are. I button up my blouse.

We go up to the room; it's simple and clean with white walls and two chaste-looking twin beds with speckled covers that match the same blue of the curtains. A few paintings of sailing boats hang above the tiny desk. I let out a chuckle.

Two single beds. You see? The receptionist's revenge for the little spectacle downstairs.

— Goddammit.

But it's a room with a view, and the sea and the horizon belong to us from our balcony. The beachcomber's bodies look like ants now, they've recovered a smidgeon of dignity. Santi, a builder to the bitter end, incapable of leaving a space be if there's a way to make it better, takes one of the mattresses out onto the balcony, lays me down and starts undressing me. It's so bright I can hardly see him. I close my eyes and my head starts to spin. I open them and try to concentrate on his kisses, moving up along my legs, but I'm feeling woozy and all I want is for him to bring a glass of water.

— You're really pale. Do you feel OK? he asks.

I take two sips and start to gag. I want to get up, but can't stand on my own, so Santi walks me over to the bathroom and I throw up until there is not a solid thing left. I continue retching liquid, and once I've got rid of all the alcohol, my body remains staunchly devoted to expelling whatever else it can, just in case. My body – yet another paradise lost. I finally compose myself and stop heaving. I catch sight of our reflection in the mirror, my naked body like a grey spirit with glassy eyes and, behind me, Santi all dressed up, the cyclist-skier, he of the red jeans, who can drink and do drugs to no end and never lose his composure, although later he needs all sorts of stimulants and can't sleep without smoking a joint or taking a sleeping pill. I'm crazy about my asymmetrical body, it's soft, skinny, imperfect and disproportionate; I spoil it, I grope it, I give it what it asks for, I follow it all over the place, I meekly obey it, I never contradict it. It's the opposite of a temple. I have tried, I have tried and never succeeded, just let my head be a temple, but my body always remains an amusement park.

— Feeling any better? Santi asks.

He passes a damp towel over my forehead and neck. He brings me my clothes.

— More or less.

— I forgot how badly you react to drinking on an empty stomach. I really wanted to spend time with you.

— Don't worry, it's my fault. That last gin and tonic was a very bad idea. If I don't die tonight, I'll be fine by the morning.

Santi loads his bike onto my car and takes me home. I open the passenger window and close my eyes. I'm exhausted; all I want to do is sleep. When we get to the front door, he hurries a goodbye peck on the lips.

— There are a lot of schools in this part of town; I could run into someone I know, he explains, looking around. And before he staggers away, he adds: — Some friends have invited us to Cadaqués, so I'm going up with my family for a few days. I'll let you know if I can sneak away at some point so we can hook up.

I close the door and rush up the stairs as fast as I can. I think I'm going to be sick again. I head straight for the bathroom.

5

The main entrance of my house is jam-packed with boxes. The maid helped me line them up along the left wall, six rows that reach almost to the ceiling, next to the boxes from my last move nearly two years ago, which I haven't even opened yet. When we came here to live, we opened boxes until there was no room left to fit a pin, not another book, not another toy, and then we just stopped. They're all downstairs now, waiting for the day we have a bigger apartment. I can't imagine what's in them. Books I suppose. At times I've looked for things and have never been able to find them. I'm sure that when the day comes, some two or twenty years hence, we'll open the boxes and find all sorts of treasures. Yours are filled with books, china, tea sets and linens. It hasn't been easy for me to part with your things, especially the ones I know you loved. There were days when I thought I would get rid of everything, and five minutes later I'd regret it and want to store every last piece of junk. Three hours later, I would rethink it all and determine to give some things away as gifts. I guess it was my way of figuring out how far away from you I wanted to live. It's a tough balance to strike; it's easier to keep a distance with the people who are alive. There's a tall coat rack next to the wall of boxes where guests used to leave their things when we threw parties. Your greyish-blue woollen jacket is hanging there now, the one with the brick-coloured stripes. It's the only article of your clothing I've kept. Not because it's a good one, but because we bought it together at your favourite shop and I saw you wear it a thousand times. I haven't had the guts to take it to the cleaner's yet. I guess it still has your smell, though I haven't been able to check on that, either. I'm a little frightened by the thing; it's like a dusty ghost covered in dog hair that says hello to me when I walk through the door. I'm still afraid of the dead. When I saw you dead I wasn't afraid, though, I would have been able to stay there sitting beside you for centuries. It was as if you simply weren't there any more, as if the light of the summer morning streaming through the window had nothing in its way, it spilled over the room, over the world, and what remained was merely our residue, your grimace of pain, the silence, the fatigue and a new-found loneliness, bottomless – as if new floors were opening below my feet as they brushed along, one after the other, welcoming me. If your soul, or something like that, survives, it got the hell out of that depressing room, and I don't blame you for it, I'm sure mine would have done the same.

— What's with the scuzzy jacket? Sofía asks when she walks through the door. She's wearing one of her mother's old hippy dresses, white linen with red piping. She took it to the seamstress a while ago and turned it into something fresh, graceful and stylish. Sofía dresses fastidiously and with an attention to detail that's unusual nowadays – I know of only a few older gentlemen who still dress so meticulously – and completely opposite my own choice of uniform, which is composed of faded jeans and men's shirts. I had already spotted the seemingly loopy, impeccably dressed eccentric one afternoon at the main entrance of our children's junior school, even before we became friendly. She showed up wearing a massive wide-brimmed hat to protect herself from the rain, and the next day she had on woollen fuchsia shorts over a black leotard and leggings. We fell into an immediate platonic crush, the teenage-girl kind, when you meet someone who not only shares the same loves and hates, your passion for white wine and your quirky way of never taking anything seriously, but who has the same way of throwing herself wholeheartedly into life and everything that comes with it – the result of a passionate character and a protected childhood.

— It's my mum's jacket, I declare. — I haven't taken it to the cleaner's yet. I'm not sure what I'm going to do with it, in any case, it's the only piece of her clothing I've kept.

I go on to describe the last time I saw Elenita, who was Marisa, my nanny's daughter. Marisa was an extraordinary woman and my second mother. She died of a heart attack two years ago. Elenita was suffering from cancer and already very ill when she greeted me wearing one of her mother's flower-patterned housecoats. I recognised it the second she opened the door, and thought how logical that she would wear it, though it also seemed like a terrible fore-shadowing for the embrace of death. And I also recall how a friend from school many years earlier, a tall and lanky girl with blonde hair, had shown me her yellow socks before running out onto the sports field one day. They had belonged to her father, who had just died of cancer, and reached all the way up to her knees. I was a virgin to death then, and it just seemed so sad and so romantic to me (as a teenager, compassion was as volatile and flickering a feeling as any other). A year later, when I turned sixteen, my father died of cancer. And from then on the dead form a sort of chain, a macabre necklace that weighs a ton, and whose last, closing link will be me, I guess.

— I think you should have it cleaned and then store it on the highest shelf in the cupboard, Elisa says. You'll decide what to do with it later, there's no hurry.

Elisa had come for lunch too, though the three of us rarely hang out at the same time – threesomes never work, not even in friendship.

— Let me go ahead and mix our cocktails now – that'll make you feel better, Sofía says.

Sofía is an expert cocktail maker and can be seen strolling around the city with an exquisite ecru-coloured canvas bag loaded with the items necessary for preparing them. Elisa has brought the sushi. I pull some dried-out leftover crumbs of cheese from the fridge, and we sit down at the table. We toast to life, to ourselves and to summertime. Lately, everyone seems hell-bent on raising a glass with me to toast something or other, summoning some future I'm not sure will ever arrive.

— Well, girls, I say, — I've decided to go to Cadaqués for a few days. Sex, drugs and rock 'n' roll. Who wants to join me?

Elisa looks at me with trepidation, and Sofía applauds the decision enthusiastically.

— Yes! That's it, let's go to Cadaqués! she exclaims while Elisa launches a scholarly discussion on the effects of drugs, Freud, grief and the maternal figure – great dangers that are stalking me. One is committed to enjoying life and the other to suffering and analysing it.

— Have you noticed how she dresses like a Cuban now that she's dating one? Sofía whispers.

— You're totally right . . .

Elisa is wearing a white flared short skirt, her flip-flops have a platform heel and her top is covered in red polka dots. Her long, dusky cloud of undulating hair is loose and there's red varnish on her finger- and toenails. She seems as happy and pert as a five-year-old. We all look younger when we're happy, but in Elisa's case, she can go from five to five thousand in a two-minute flash. She's almost never in between; when she's older, she's going to have the face of a shrewd squirrel, I think, as she continues talking with a news anchor's gravitas.

— With an arse like that, it was only a matter of time before a Cuban got a hold of her, Sofía goes on, using her inside voice.

The problem with Elisa, I tell myself, is that underneath that gorgeous Cuban arse, or more like above it, there's a brilliant and highly analytical French existentialist philosopher's mind that never sleeps, and that makes her life a tad complicated. The poor thing, she's always trying to balance her Cuban arse with her French philosopher's head.

— You should come with us, and bring the Cuban too, I say when she finally finishes.

— I've told you a thousand times, his name is Damián, she answers.

— Oh, right, Damián, Damián, Damián. I always forget. Sorry. He is Cuban though, isn't he? The only one I know.

Elisa looks at me earnestly and doesn't say a word. My relationships with my friends are always impassioned and often a little troubled, though it's subsided a bit with my mother's illness. I wonder how long it will take for them to go back to the way they were.

— Yeah, why don't you come with us? Sofía exclaims. How's it going with Damián, anyway? Are you happy?

— Yes, but he's very demanding sexually. Truth be told, I'm exhausted.

Elisa can turn any subject, even sex with her new

boyfriend, into something brainy and intellectual. Sofía, on the other hand, turns everything into the frivolous and festive, and inevitably everything revolves around her. Each one of us carries our own leitmotif in life, a common strand, a motto, a signature fragrance that envelops us, a background music that accompanies us wherever we go, abiding, silenced every now and then, but enduring and imperishable.

— Who else is coming? Sofía asks.

— Let me think. Oh, um, yeah, my two ex-husbands!

— What? they both cry in unison.

— You're going to Cadaqués with both of your exes? Are you joking? And you think that's normal? Elisa says.

— I don't know if it's normal. But you both spend all day telling me I shouldn't be alone, that I should surround myself with the people who care about me. Well, I think both Oscar and Guillem love me.

— I think it's a great idea, Sofía says. Normal is boring. Let's drink to being abnormal.

— Here's to being abnormal! I shout and we hug.

When Sofía's had a few too many, she starts kissing and declaring eternal love to whomever is sitting closest to her.

— Oh, and Santi will be there too. With his family, I add quickly.

This time even Sofía looks at me dubiously.

— It's going to be fun – just wait and see.

They both stare at me with eyes like dinner plates. I laugh.

6

Taking off for Cadaqués is always a sort of expedition. The three children are sitting in the back seat, Edgar, Nico and Daniel, Sofía's boy, together with Úrsula, the babysitter. I'm driving and Sofía occupies the co-pilot's seat. It still seems bizarre and even a little absurd that I should be at the head of the excursion, the person who decides what time to leave, who gives Úrsula her instructions, who picks out the clothes the children will wear, who drives the car. At any moment, I think, as I peer through the rear-view mirror and catch the children fighting and laughing at the same time, someone's going take my mask off and send me back there with them, where I belong. I'm a total fraud at being an adult, my efforts to progress beyond the playground at break time have all been resounding failures. I feel as if I'm still six years old, I see the same things, the little jumping dog whose head appeared and disappeared from the frame of a ground-floor window, a grandfather holding out his hand for his grandson, handsome men with their radar on, the charms on my bracelet reflecting rays of sunlight, lonely old men, couples locked in ardent kisses, beggars, suicidal old ladies crossing the street at a turtle's pace, trees. Each of us sees different things, but we always see the same things, and what we see defines us absolutely. Instinctively, we love other people who see the same things that we do, and we recognise each other immediately. Place a man in the middle of a street and ask him: 'What do you see?' It'll all be there, in the way he responds, like in a fairy tale. What we think isn't so important; it's what we see that really counts. I'd hand in this pathetic cardboard crown of adulthood without thinking twice – I wear it so ungracefully anyway, it's constantly falling off and rolling down the street – if only to be once again sitting in the back seat next to my brother Bruno, with Marisa the nanny and Elenita, who always joined us on holidays, our two dachshunds Sapho and Corina, and Lali, Marisa's giant poodle, that ungainly, flea-bitten, hysterical dog who hated Cadaqués and the refinement of our own dogs.

— Hey, boys, what do you say we buy a ping-pong table for the garage in Cadaqués?

They all readily approve the idea.

— But you have to be careful of the dogs and the ping-pong table, OK?

— Why? What for? Nico and Daniel ask at the same time. Edgar, like a typical teenager, is messing around with his mobile not saying a word, though I can tell he's paying attention, he always is.

So I tell them how Marisa's psychopathic dog Lali used to have these sudden hyperactive fits in Cadaqués when she'd bolt off, galloping full speed down the stairs, while Elenita, Marisa and I chased after her shouting and trying to catch her. She'd be practically at the garage, when she'd jump out into the open space of the stairwell that was some four metres down, and crash-land onto the ping-pong table where my brother and his friends would be peacefully hanging out and playing. The sudden shock of such a huge black dog crashing into the table sent the children running in all directions, terrified, and as the summer advanced, Bruno was left without ping-pong pals. He was convinced that it was me who taught Lali to throw herself down the stairwell and onto the ping-pong table, just to annoy him.

— Yeah, right, Edgar says, looking at me sideways. — Grandma used to say, 'Bad, Blanca, you're so bad.'

— Grandma never said that, I lie.

— She said it every time she saw you.

— She was just joking. Grandma adored me.

— Yeah, sure.

Grandma was frightened; the fearless woman began living in fear when her strength began to fail her, followed by her head, her friends, the entourage who always hovered around her ('Know what one of the toughest things about growing old is?' she asked me one day. 'Realising that nobody cares what you have to say.'), when she saw that her time was winding down, that everything was coming to an end, everything, that is, except her eager desire to live. Grandma never gave up – she fought every battle and was accustomed to winning. She never accepted that the game was over until the very last day. I told her not to worry once, sitting on the bed with her in the final hospital, a place I still visit in my nightmares (though not as often as the assisted-living home where she had spent the previous two months, where I learned how realistic the films are about the living dead, the directors don't make that stuff up). It was her third bout of pneumonia, she'd recover from this one too, I told her. I'll be fine, don't worry, the children will be fine, everything's in order. She looked at me and didn't say a word, she couldn't speak any more – what sort of dying person is in the mood to utter a last sentence? I guess the ones concerned with posterity, though maybe all the fuss about a person's last words is just another load of nonsense – then she started to cry, without making a noise, without moving a single muscle of her face, just staring straight at me. Ana, her best friend, was in the room at the time and I suppose to protect me she said it must be the air conditioning irritating her eyes. But I know you were saying goodbye to me. I didn't shed a tear, just squeezed your hand gently and told you again to just be calm, we're all fine. A few months earlier, when your death was still something inconceivable to me, and still is now, we were at your house chatting. Suddenly, out of nowhere, you stood up to get something from the bathroom and said, without even glancing over at me and as nonchalantly as someone saying 'I need some toothpaste', that 'it's been an honour to know you'. I made you repeat it twice; at that time our love had grown painful, I thought you didn't love me and I wasn't sure if I still loved you. So I burst into tears, told you not to say such silly things, and within two minutes we were back to fighting again. I think you already knew by then that the time of the ellipses, the suspension points you hated so much, was coming to an end. Here we are now at the full stop, like a dagger, like an oxygen cylinder.

Elisa waves contentedly from the other lane, in her own car with Damián. I watch them and feel a little jealous pang. I imagine them listening to music – the music they want, not what the children want to hear – talking and thinking things over. I also imagine how Elisa, who doesn't have kids, must have showered alone, or maybe with Damián, certainly without a child and his chirpy babysitter barging in to ask the whereabouts of his Chinese costume, he absolutely has to bring it because in Cadaqués either one goes dressed as a Mandarin, or one doesn't go at all. 'End of story.' Nico added. 'I'm naked and in the shower, you can see that, right? Get out of here!' Nico whined and Úrsula couldn't help laughing at him, which is her technique for coping with any situation. My second husband found it unnerving, but it has always amused me. 'Lightness is a form of elegance', I used to say. 'To live with grace and joy is extremely difficult.' 'You mistake lightness with indifference, Blanquita. Everyone pulls the wool over your eyes,' he said.

We decided to stop for lunch at Tom's house to take a break on the way, which is near the halfway point. Tom, Daniel's father, and Sofía had been romantically involved when they were younger, and though the relationship ended, they remained close friends. When Sofía realised that she was still unattached and getting closer to the age when having a child would become more and more difficult, she decided to ask him to help her make one. Tom had got married in the meantime, had two daughters and then separated. He made it very clear that the child could have his last name and that he would see him from time to time, but that it would be Sofía's child to raise, and only hers, since he already had two daughters whom he actively parented and couldn't be responsible for any more. Sofía gratefully accepted the agreement, aware of the gift it represented, and Tom got on with his life.

He now lives in a ramshackle house in the middle of a huge plot of land, where he runs a shelter for dogs and breeds beagles. If I were someone else, one of my dreams would be to live in the countryside surrounded by animals, but I get anxious if I don't have a cinema, a twenty-four-hour corner shop and a load of strangers in my vicinity. Anyway, I am as excited as the children at the chance to

see a litter of puppies. And the break comes as an unex-
pected relief from the road to Cadaqués, which we'll go
back to again soon enough. It still hurts to drive along
the roads I used to take with my mother; the 'bitch of
death' expels us from so many familiar places. Maybe we
should keep one of the beagle puppies, I think, as we
make our way down the long, quiet, lonely dirt road that
leads to Tom's house. A dusty green sign with sprightly
dogs announces 'Villa Beagle'. We ring the bell and there's
no answer. The children perch on the fence and start to
yell 'Tom! Tom!' There's the sound of barking in the
distance, and suddenly a whole pack of dogs trots towards
us, expressing all ages, races and conditions. Whenever I
see these animals enjoying their freedom, even if only for
a moment, invented and domesticated as they are by
humans and used to living confined in apartments, it
immediately puts me in a good mood. To see their un-
bridled joy at dashing in the sun, ears flapping in the
wind, tongues hanging, tails wagging excitedly. It's the
thrill of being alive, nothing more than that, of accepting
that gift without questioning it. The dogs crowd in a
tangle around the other side of the fence and the children
squeal, unable to contain their excitement. Behind the
dogs, two smiling boys approach the gate. They walk
with relaxed strides, as if they were opening a trail through
a field of tall wheat, dressed in worn jeans, looking a little
sleepy, the elastic silhouettes of youth, with the trouble-
maker's mischievous look in their eyes, from spending

plenty of time on the street, skipping school. I watch them amused, and with a tinge of envy, as they discreetly pass a joint between themselves and call out to each one of the dogs by their name, frolicking around with them. They finally open the gate to let us in and tell us that Tom is in the house, that he just woke up and he's on his way. The dogs greet us cheerfully, jumping, licking and letting out an occasional bark that is immediately reprimanded by one of the boys. The children have never seen so many dogs in a single place, so they're a little apprehensive at first, but within a few minutes they're running around the field, laughing and screaming, with the dogs springing and bounding behind. There's one of them, though, that doesn't leave my side. He's an old, scruffy thing vaguely reminiscent of a German shepherd. He was the first dog I noticed, hanging at the back of the group, a little detached, with a tired, sad look in his eyes. He saw that I'd noticed him, and so he approached me directly. Anyone who's had a dog knows that they choose us, and not the other way round. It's the same type of recognition that can happen, on rare occasions, between two people. A sort of mute, immediate, undeniable acknowledgement. But in the case of a dog, it lasts a lifetime. I pet his head and every time I remove my hand, he brings his snout to my leg and gives me little nudges to ask for more pampering.

— What's his name? I ask one of the boys.

— Rey.

— Of course. I bet at some point in his life, for someone, he was a king.

The tall, lanky boy smiles and passes me the joint without even asking.

— His owner died of cancer a few months ago, and he came here.

I kneel and caress his head again.

— You're still a king to me. You know that? You can tell from a mile away. You've been abandoned too, huh? Well, well. Life's a bitch, isn't it?

I give him a few pats on the back; his coat is strong, robust, a little scratchy, black, and reddish-blond along his belly and legs. He has the boundless, sombre and clouded gaze of an old dog, like that of a sick man's. If you like people, it's impossible not to like dogs.

In the distance, Edgar inspects the fig trees that border the meadow with the air of a landowner. They're laden with fruit that's bursting ripe. He'll never be so adult, I think, so conscious of everything around him, so serious, kind, discreet, so frugal with his words, so sensitive and responsible, as he is now at thirteen. I'll never catch up with him, that's for sure. Perhaps respect is the highest feeling you can have towards another person, more than love or adoration. Damián comes up to me and asks me in a whisper to pass the joint, Elisa doesn't like him to smoke. Sofía is flirting with the other young dog trainer, who turns out is Romanian and hardly speaks any Spanish. Roger, the one who is talking to me, is Catalan, and while we smoke he explains that aside from sheltering abandoned dogs, they also have a kennel to keep people's pets when they have to travel or go on holiday and don't have anyone who can look after them. That's when Tom shows up. He obviously dressed in a rush, – he's wearing torn trousers.

— Your arse is showing, Sofía greets him.

He touches the seat of his trousers and lets out a snigger. He speaks Spanish with a posh accent from Barcelona, and Catalan like a peasant from the Empordan. His British mother is to blame for his honey-coloured hair, and blue, romantic eyes, and he has the typical build of a Southern man: a square body, strong and stocky, with squat, pudgy hands, and brown, sun-wrinkled skin. He's upfront and always looks a person in the eye when talking, probably something he picked up from the dogs. He has an easy laugh; he's vigorous and knows how to take charge. He likes animals, women, poker and dope. According to Sofía, he has a plantation that stretches a few kilometres beyond the kennels, which is what finances the animal shelter, among other things.

We decide to go and see the puppies before having lunch. We cross a field of fig and olive trees and reach a low building that's divided into cubicles; some are outside and full of puppies, who bobble and wriggle around like mad when they hear us approaching, and others, the newborns, are just inside a shaded courtyard where it's cooler and calmer, removed from the bustle of the older dogs. Something solemn floats in the atmosphere, the wonder that always accompanies birth, whether it be human or animal. There's that fanciful yet nonetheless overwhelming feeling of almost being able to brush the very beginning of things with the tips of your fingers, the eternal bliss. The children can perceive the fatigue, the surrender, the abandon of the mothers who have recently given birth, the disorientated, fragile little puppies, blind and ugly as hairless mice, the nauseating smell of life, and they keep quiet without daring to enter. They ask me to bring one of the older puppies over to them. I consider keeping one of the puppies and giving her your name, and immediately realise it's just the kind of idea I'd have after smoking dope and that I should never have smoked on an empty stomach. I tell the children they should ask Santa Claus to bring them a puppy.

We decide to go and have lunch at a small roadside hotel, a pleasant and simple place, unpretentious, but with very good home cooking, the kind I never had at home when I was growing up. You told me once that when the time for bottles and baby food came to an end, you went to see our paediatrician to ask about nutrition. He was a prominent figure in the field, an attractive and imposing wise man who terrified me – he kicked me out of his consulting room once for crying. You explained that you'd never once set foot in a kitchen, and that you had no intention of doing so now. Dr Sauleda told you not to worry, that with some milk or other lactic products in the fridge, some fruit, biscuits and maybe a little boiled ham, everything would be fine. So we became experts in French cheese well before puberty, and the importance of always having a bottle of champagne on hand, just in case, and it seemed the most normal thing in the world that dinner some nights would be no more than a cake from Sacha, our favourite bakery. Our kitchen was there to heat food when we had guests over, and for the girl to prepare that disgusting boiled rice with liver your dogs liked so much, until they were forced to eat only dry food along with the rest of the canine race. Dr Sauleda must have been right, though, because we both grew up to be rather attractive young people, strong, healthy and tall, refined enough to consider – and for me it's still the case – that there's nothing in the world more exotic and succulent than home cooking. We'd literally devour lentils at our friends' homes when invited over for dinner, Cuban-style rice or macaroni gulped down before the astonished and flattered gaze of our hosts, as if they were the tastiest dishes in the world.

After lunch, the children and Úrsula take a dip in the pool while the rest of us have coffee on the terrace. They bring us a bottle of ratafia liquor, a local herb digestif, and little glasses to serve ourselves. Tom is a regular there and has his rituals. He tells us about an important poker tournament he's been invited to.

— My mother loved to play poker, I say.

— Why don't you ask her to join us?

That someone could possibly not know that my mother is dead seems to me as far-fetched as not knowing the earth is round.

— She's dead. She died thirty-four days ago.

He looks at me surprised and unsmiling. I feel like blurting out 'Ehhh, gotcha! I'm just pulling your leg. Mum is fine, as insufferable as ever.'

— Oh, I'm so sorry, I had no idea.

— She tried to teach me how to play poker a million times.

— Well, maybe I can teach you.

— Yeah, that would be great.

Tom has just broken up with his girlfriend – some New Ager nut living up in the mountains according to Sofía – and his radar is on. Some men don't have a sexual radar, or they hardly ever use it, only when they need to, and then they turn it off. Others have it on permanently, even when they're sleeping; in the supermarket checkout queue, in front of a computer screen, in the waiting room at the dentist, spinning round and round, sending and receiving signals. Civilisation exists thanks to the first category, and the world thanks to the second.

— Why don't we go and see a film? Sofía suggests suddenly.

We've drunk a little too much, and we all think it's a good idea to wait a while before getting back on the road.

— Sure, yeah, Tom says. He looks at me and says: — We can sit next to each other and play footsie.

We crack up. And even though I'm not really attracted to him, I flirt away anyway. And I feel the honey start to flow, all liquid and sunny, two kids about to steal a bag of sweets and run from the shop laughing and feeling frightened all at the same time. It's not the thick kind of honey, the slow, dark variety, the kind you would go straight to hell for, but it's honey all the same, an antidote against death. Ever since you died, and even for a while before that, I've felt as if all I do is plunder love, take off with the slightest crumb of it I find in my path, like hoarding little nuggets of gold. I'm completely ruined and I need someone to steal what's left, relieve the weight. Even the smile of the cashier in the supermarket, the wink of a stranger on the street, a trite conversation with the newsagent, I make use of everything, there's never enough, and nothing ever works.

The film is about a boy whose dog is hit by a car and killed, but his young owner miraculously resuscitates him, only to die again and be resuscitated one last time. We sit in two rows, the adults in front and the children and Úrsula behind us. Tom grasps my hand and we spend the whole film that way; he kisses it once very discreetly and brushes my neck with his lips. I rest my head on his shoulder and close my eyes for a few seconds. He caresses my knee; I let him, it's nice but not electrifying, we're both just there. Maybe there has to be a minimum amount of desire before you attain something. We both cry at the end of the film and we both pretend to hide it. I haven't been this civilised with a man for a long time. The children have a great time and now they want a dog more than ever. We return to Tom's house as the sun begins to set and Edgar asks permission to pick a few ripe figs. The stray dogs run through the prairie stepping on the last rays of light filtered through trees and clouds. Rey comes near to greet me parsimoniously, the old, dethroned flea-bitten monarch.

— Why don't you keep him? Tom says. — He's a good dog. He likes you. No wonder.

— I like him too. But I don't know, I think the children might prefer a puppy. None of the dogs I've ever lived with have been truly mine – either they belonged to my mother or one of my exes. My mother said I was incapable of taking care of a dog. I admire what you're doing here; the fiends who abandon their dogs should be thrown in jail.

— Thanks. Well, if you change your mind some day, you know where he is.

He hands us a rolled-up plastic bag tied in numerous knots before we head off. Sofía opens it, laughs and shows it to me.

— So it's true about the plantation!

— I thought it might be nice for your holiday. See you around!

It's late by the time we get to Cadaqués and we march the sleepy children straight off to bed. I leave my friends on the terrace drinking gin and tonics and go to sleep.

Before lying down, I see that I have a missed call from Tom. I don't answer it, he must be looking for someone, but not me. I hug my pillow. I ask it for a quiet night, although I know I won't get one. There's a howling deep inside that usually leaves me well enough alone by day, but at night, when I lie in bed and try to sleep, it rouses and begins snuffling around like an angry cat, scratching my chest, tightening my jaw, hammering at my temples. Sometimes, to appease it, I open my mouth and pretend to scream in silence, but I'm never able to fool it, it stays there, frenzied, trying to break me. The dawn, the children, the modesty of everyday tasks, soothe and tame it for a few hours, but then night falls once more and I'm alone, and here it comes again, right on time for our rendezvous. I close my eyes hard. I open them. It's back.

7

I wake up early the next morning and go up to the terrace
to look out over the Mediterranean. Memories tangle into
a tight blanket that for once doesn't smother me. I guess
that's what an ancestral home is for, a place in which
everyone's lived at one time or another, where everything's
happened. Life, our life, was such a privileged one. My
grandfather used to bring boxes of fruit up from Barcelona,
Remei would carry the dirty clothes to be washed, Pepita
de la Galiota would bring huge batches of custard pudding
to our house on trays, there was Marisa's gazpacho, and
the eternal bread-and-butter breakfasts, the railing
bedecked in a colourful garland of drying beach towels,
the naps that were taken only reluctantly, dressing up to
go into town, the afternoon ice cream, archery practice.
Then the first time we got tipsy, the first loves, the first
sunrises, the first drugs – sliding through the silky water
after dropping acid, the characters in the paintings hanging
in the living room coming to life and turning into

monsters, dancing at dawn in the deserted town square with a girlfriend until we ran into a tree – nights without sleeping, wild laughter, the excitement of never knowing what was going to happen, the absolute certainty that the world belonged to us. And when I learned what a boyfriend was for, boyfriends. When I conceived my first son. Coming to Cadaqués with the children. The children cracking their heads open against the sharp architectural styles of the seventies, as my brother had done every summer, decades earlier. And then came the separations. Your dotage, when the doors to the house that had forever been thrown wide for everyone – even at night they were left open – started closing, pressed shut by some invisible wind. And happiness, little by little, stopped being what it was despite the unbroken routine of breakfast, boat, lunch, nap and games of cards. And seeing my drinking buddies now all with children and a haggard look in their eyes. When you're young, even though you're exhausted, your eyes never take on a weary expression; there are days now when I can't even lift my gaze from the ground. And then Marisa's death. And then her daughter Elenita's a few years later. And I felt obliged to accompany you to Cadaqués for a few days, even though I didn't really feel like it, and then, nothing. I watched the house grow old with you, be left alone and then, become you. And yet, there's the pinkish-white light of the morning, the gossamer air and the sparkling calm of the sea that belie all the world's tragedies and strive to announce that we are happy and that we have it all. If I don't look back, it could almost seem as though life were just beginning – the landscape is almost identical to when I was twenty. I look up at your bedroom, the most spacious and beautiful room of the house, with the best views. Every once in a while you'd station yourself at the top of the stairs with your wild grey hair, wearing one of your long, threadbare summer tunics – bought by the maids at the street fair, since you didn't care to pick them out yourself, so sure that elegance is a state of mind, not an aesthetic – and from here you looked like a general leading his troops, all day long telling everyone what to do. Sometimes we'd be on the terrace swinging in the hammocks and chatting quietly, when suddenly you'd butt in with some hilarious or wicked comment from your bedroom. Nobody uses your room any more; maybe I'll let Guillem stay there with Patum. I just can't go in there.

I leave the house before the others wake up – I need coffee and I'd like to visit the cemetery. The town is full of summer visitors, but it still seems quiet at this hour, when the early risers are buying bread and the newspaper, planning lunch before taking off to sail or doing chores with their children. Mornings in which the most important decision of the day is what to have for lunch, and don't forget the children's sunscreen. There are nearly no young people in the street at this hour. I guess they're all sleeping. I miss that about being young, being able to sleep so soundly. Now when I get into bed it's as if I were lying down in my coffin. Some days, I fall asleep curled up on the couch to avoid that feeling. Finding sex is relatively easy, finding someone who will hold you through the night is another thing altogether, it's different, and not even that is a guarantee for a peaceful night's sleep; some men can be very uncomfortable. The warm morning breeze ruffles my ricepaper-thin silk dress, which swells and floats lightly atop my skin. How to be rid of the weight and how to reduce the burden of other things, when sadness makes everything weigh two tons? At the news-stand in the square I've been going to since I was a little girl, the owners offer their condolences, again, discreetly, and almost apologetically. I appreciate it when people don't make a spectacle of their sympathy, or solidarity, though with love it's more difficult to do, there's something fluorescent about young lovers, as if they existed smack in the eye of a vortex, and no wind could pull them away. We're never as formidable as when we're in love and our love is reciprocated. At least in my case it's an experience that sets the bar so high that only the brief spark of sex can offer any substitute; low-intensity love doesn't do the trick, because it doesn't exist. As I'm walking along I run across Joan, the mayor, dressed in navy-blue Bermudas and an impeccably white shirt. He's tanned and always seems to be happy. We've known each other since we were kids, and he responded very kindly when I wrote to let him know that you wanted to be buried here. He said yes, that he could arrange everything, and that as long as there's life, nothing is lost. I knew that everything was perfectly lost, but I thanked him for his words and support. I think you're buried in one of the most beautiful places on earth and some day, soon, now that I can still look death in the face from the pedestal of good health and forty years of age, I'll buy the niche next to yours. You can see the sunrise from there; we won't even have to get up.

Joan is handsome, well mannered and seductive, even a little too sexy to be a politician. Whenever I see him, I ask if he's truly the Mayor of Cadaqués. It always cracks him up. Flirting moves in mysterious ways. The idea that one of my friends is now mayor seems outrageous and totally incompatible with my idea that we're all still in the playground at break time, skipping around and staring at the clouds. My father used to say that being the Mayor of Cadaqués has to be the best job on earth, although I never actually heard him say it, you were the one who told me. I don't remember ever being with him in Cadaqués, I was so little when you separated. Most of what I know about him, I learned from you. I remember one day when I was visiting at the last home you were in, the one they expelled you from for bad behaviour: really it was the Parkinson's devouring your brain and the dyke had a hole in it, and without your extraordinary head controlling things, the floodwaters came pouring in. Truth be told, by then you were already too ill to live in that luxury assisted-living place for the elderly, even though you insisted that it wasn't true out of rage and desperation, more rage than anything else. I tried to reason with you, told you it was time to hand over your weapons, stop refusing our help, that if this is the end, let's do it right, like we always said we would, with dignity, calmly and in peace. And I gave my father as an example of his fortitude before illness and death. They said – you said – that one day in the hospital, when he was already very ill, he commented, 'Considering how life is a bitch, mine has been pretty good.' And from the shadows you answered me: 'Your father's death wasn't like that, not like what you think.'

I didn't have the courage to ask then how had it been. And you didn't say anything else, just left that poisoned sentence hovering between us, you stabbed me with it, and I couldn't tell if in a fit of lucidity or of madness. Now I'll never know, and I don't want to know if Dad died screaming, terrified, or with the heroic dignity that helped the stupid little girl I was then, live better for so many years.

I walk into the Maritim to have breakfast and find all the regulars at the habitual tables – the tourists all sit at the edge of the beach – close to the glass dividers that provide shelter from the wind, and allow a view of the people who come and go, like that beautiful, mysterious stranger who was at your funeral. I recognise him instantly, that great and formidable head, his lively, quick gaze that gives away a touch of the jocose, his chestnut beard and blonder hair, all thick and tousled, his big nose and plump lips camouflaged by the beard, and long, lean but solid build. He's poring over the newspaper but looks up when he notices that someone is approaching. A smile escapes my lips and we both immediately look the other way. Anyway, I'm not really in the mood for more condolences, or to impose my own sadness and exhaustion on a stranger. And yet, I can feel myself perk up; I remove my sunglasses and pull the hem of my dress up just a tad. I think I share with most other women on the planet, and maybe the Pope or some other religious leader too, the wild idea that love is the only thing that can save us. Men, and some clever women, know that work, ambition, effort and curiosity can also save us. But I believe that nobody can live without a minimum effective dose of love and physical contact. There's a point below which we begin to rot. Prostitutes are essential; and there should be prostitutes of love, too. But love is too difficult to reproduce, and faking it properly is too labour-intensive, long and subversive. Not to mention ruinous.

— Who are you flirting with now? Sofia asks, as she plops down next to me and places her huge straw hat on another chair.

— Why do you think I'm flirting?

— You're assuming your trademark flirting position: perky, straight-backed and sinuous. And your knickers are showing.

I giggle. — That's not true. And it's my swimsuit.

— Oh, but I think it's just fine. And turning to the waiter, who is carrying a tray laden with croissants and buttered toast: — Would you bring me a draught beer, please? A little one. And she measures a minuscule size with her forefinger and thumb. — I'm a little hung-over.

I watch her from the corner of my eye, so tiny, with her pleated shorts, striped shirt and butterfly glasses. She has her dark hair as impeccably combed as always; she washes, dries and irons it every day, wherever she is. Her skin is uniformly brown. Her mouth perfectly shaped with a tiny freckle on the upper lip. She has expressive eyes and a lean, wiry body that is well proportioned.

— Remember what I said about a beautiful man I didn't know being at the funeral?

— Yeah, I remember.

— Well, he's here.

— Get out. She looks around with the type of frenetic expression one imagines an ornithologist would have after being told there's a long-extinct bird crossing the sky. A smile crosses her face. — I know which one he is. The one over there, sitting beside the glass divider. Do I know you to a T or what?

I giggle again. — How'd you guess?

— Easy. He has all your favourite features: big nose, strong but lean body, the relaxed elegance of people who feel comfortable anywhere. Simplicity. His worn, faded T-shirt and espadrilles. Holes in his jeans. He's not out to prove anything, no outward displays, no bracelets, tattoos, caps or expensive watches. He's your type. Why don't you go and say hello?

— You're nuts. No way, I'd die of embarrassment. He might not even remember me. I wasn't at my best the day of the funeral.

— What do you mean? You were gorgeous; though you seemed sad and self-absorbed, which hasn't changed much since then.

— It's called depression, I answer. — I wonder why he was there at all, if he knew my mother.

— Why don't you just go over and ask?

— No, it doesn't matter, some other time.

— Are you sure there'll be another time?

— There's always another time. Well, maybe not always. But I'm sure this one lives here.

— Right. You're just chicken.

Just then the beautiful stranger gets up. Sofía nudges me with her elbow and we both stare at him, speechless. He takes a few steps towards the exit, looks over in our direction, stops and nods a timid farewell. Sofía responds waving her hand effusively as if she were waving goodbye to thousands of passengers on a huge transatlantic cruise ship.

— Now listen, if you don't pick him up, I will.

— That's just perfect.

Just then, Guillem calls to let me know he'll be arriving the following day. Sofía's never met him and is curious to see what he's like. I can't imagine two more opposite people. Sofía is worldly, generous, tolerant, honest and transparent, as enthusiastic as she is infantile, impassioned and narcissistic. And Guillem is the most sarcastic, ironic and unpretentious man I know. His principles are carved in stone and he has zero patience for nonsense. Sofía is capable of calling me first thing in the morning to tell me she hadn't slept a wink all night, she's in the throes of a high creative point and overwhelmed with nifty ideas on how to transform and combine garments from last season. Guillem dresses almost entirely in old T-shirts designed by his students to raise money for their class trip. She's as tiny and delicate as a porcelain doll, and though when we first met he was as skinny as our son is now, he's grown into the solid, vigorous man he was always meant to be. What we have inside always ends up expressing itself. We become what we are, beauty and youth only camouflage it for a time. Sometimes I think I catch a glimpse of the face my friends will have when they're older, though I can't yet see it in my sons, it's too early, they're still flooded by the light of life, they throb. I can hardly bear to look at my own face, only askance, and from a distance. Your face disappeared, Mum, hidden behind the mask of disease. Every day I try to see it again, jump beyond the last few years to once again encounter your true face, the way it was before it turned to stone. It's like carrying a hammer to knock down walls. Or like what happens with sadness, whose wafer-thin layers of crackling glass settle over us gradually, enshroud us little by little. We're like the little pea buried under a thousand mattresses, like a bright light flickering feebly. And only true love can end pain, like in the fairy tales, and sometimes not even then. Time soothes the ache, pacifies us, like a lion tamer.

Sofía drains her glass of beer while Elisa, who has just shown up with Damián, decides on the lunch menu. Sofía is responsible for buying the wine, and I get a pedicure since I'm in mourning, and less is expected of me in the way of domestic duties, which are usually negligible anyway. I'll go to the cemetery some other time, later in the afternoon or tomorrow morning.

There's only one pharmacy in the whole town. It's a tiny seafront place with old-fashioned charm chock-full of products and perfumes, and the slightly faded smell of talcum powder and roses. There's a tiny cabin round the back for beauty treatments. A middle-aged woman, more middle than me, does my pedicure and tells me that, aside from being a beautician, she's also a witch. I blurt out:
— I'm a witch too, and I'm witchy. Both things. I add. She remains silent and looks at me with a kind of dubious expression, squinting her eyes. She doesn't look like a witch to me. Fortunately, she's dressed like a woman from the provinces. Brown knee-length skirt, white short-sleeved shirt with a pattern design of tiny pastel-blue flowers, white nurse's clogs. She's blonde, well coiffed and painted, a little on the plump and motherly side. Though nowadays, any woman older than me seems motherly enough that I feel the desire to throw myself into their arms.

I lie back on the couch and she begins massaging my feet. I close my eyes and breathe deeply. Since your death, the only thing that alleviates me is physical contact, however fleeting or casual, or light. I've had to close all my books since I'm incapable of reading, of finding consolation in them now, they bring me back to you, your house lined with bookshelves, your meticulous annual library cleaning, vacuum cleaner in hand, our expeditions to London to find yet another treasure of children's illustrations, the hours sitting together on the bed in the hotel poring over them, I more distracted, coming and going and doing other things, you completely absorbed like a little girl.

'You can tell if someone really loves books by the way they look at them, how they open and close them, how they turn the pages,' you used to say.

Same as with men, I thought, and sometimes said. And you would look at me, half shocked, half amused, half grande dame, half woman who lost no opportunity to enjoy herself in life, and you'd laugh. We were never the type of mother and daughter who confided absolutely everything to each other, we were never friends, we never shared intimacies; I think we always tried to be a more decent version of ourselves to each other. I remember how amazed you were the day you told me that maybe you'd have to take me to see a doctor if I didn't have a period soon, and I told you nonchalantly that I'd had periods for two years now, and that I didn't say anything because I didn't think it was your business. We were in the car and you slammed the brakes, looked at me open-mouthed for a few seconds, and finally accelerated when the people behind us started honking angrily. And we never brought the subject up ever again.

I can't open a book now without thinking of you, but with men it's different. I knew from a very young age, instinctively, that I needed to keep this part of my life from you, or you might invade it too, with your ego, your generosity, your insight and your love. You watched me from afar when I fell in and out of love, take a good licking and get back on my feet. You enjoyed my happiness and let me suffer in peace, without too much of a fuss or giving too much advice. I guess you were partly aware that you were the love of my life, and no other stormy love affair would ever come close to outdoing yours. After all, we love the way we were loved in childhood, and all the love that comes afterwards is only ever a replica of that first love. I owe you, then, all my later loves, even the blind, wild love I feel for my boys. I'll never be able to open a book without wanting to see your calm, concentrated face, without knowing that I'll never see it ever again, and what is perhaps even worse is that it won't ever see me again, either. I will never be seen through your eyes again. When the world begins to depopulate of the people who love us, we become, little by little and following the rhythm of death, strangers. My place in the world was in your gaze and it was so unquestionable and perpetual that I never bothered to find out what was there. Not bad – I was able to remain a little girl until I was forty years old, with two children, two marriages, a slew of relationships, several apartments, several jobs, and now I hope I'll be able to make the transition into becoming an adult and not go straight on to old-ladyhood. I don't like being an orphan; I'm not made for this depth of sadness. Or maybe I am, maybe it's the precise size of pain, maybe it's the only dress left that can fit me.

— I can feel that you have a knot inside. There's a lot of tension here, the beautician-witch tells me. — Can I place my hands on your heart?

I reluctantly say yes. To begin with, my chest is not a place for strange middle-aged women to place their hands, I don't care if she is a witch. She places them gently, and I can feel her heat through the silk of my dress. But I can't relax, I'm too self-conscious of the intimate nature of the gesture. Thirty seconds later, she removes them.

— You're closed, hard as a rock, as if your heart were locked inside a cage.

— My mother just died, I answer.

— Ah, well. She keeps silent, which shows without a shadow of a doubt that she's a complete phoney. A real witch would have had more resources when confronted by death. — Well, she finally responds, — I have essential oils that help open the heart, you burn them at night, before sleeping –

— I'm sorry, but I really dislike that New Age stuff, I

say, interrupting, thinking I should never have let her feel my tits up. — I don't believe in natural medicine, or homeopathy, none of that stuff.

— Not even Bach flower remedies? she asks, horrified, clutching tightly at the little gold cross with a tiny ruby in the centre that she's wearing around her neck.

— No, not even that.

She looks at me with pity, apparently feeling sorrier that I don't believe in her esoteric paraphernalia than that I just lost my mother.

— My grandfather was a doctor, a surgeon, and in my house we believed in science, I apologise.

She finishes her work in silence. She looks at my feet; my toenails are like little flames. When I leave, the beautician-witch gives me two small decanters of essential oil.

— You'll see, they'll do you good. Take care now. I'll give them to the children, I think, so they can concoct their magic potions. They're the ones who really understand.

8

Elisa shows up sporting a jean miniskirt, white sleeveless top and silver sandals that just don't match. She's very tanned and her hair is down in a long, flowing cloud. She's dressed for Damián, I think a little begrudgingly. Dressing up for one particular man is very different from dressing up for men in general, or for nobody, which is how I choose my wardrobe lately. In any case, the most elegant people are those who dress for themselves. Elisa is not tall, but has a nice figure, she's thin and feminine, and everything gravitates towards that bum of hers. When I tell her I like her hands, they're thin and nervy, almost as big as mine despite our difference in height, she answers humbly, 'They're hands for getting things done.' And it's true, they're practical, realist hands, not the kind for slaying lions, like the hands of the men I like; neither are they hands for slaying souls, or for calling forth the gods and carrying old rings, like yours, Mum, although I'm sure they too can alleviate a fever and shoo nightmares away. If it weren't for Elisa, I doubt anyone would ever eat. Sofia and I will nourish ourselves by way of yogurts, toast and white wine, whatever it takes to avoid having to cook. And our children are so healthy and strong that sometimes I think all they need is a little water.

We're having dinner at Carolina and Pep's house and Hugo, Pep's best friend, who is spending a few days with them, will be coming too. Another man I flirt with dreamily while Elisa and Sofia are talking about shoes.

Edgar comes up at that moment, long and flexible, his legs and arms bronzed. Nico is still a scrumptious little puppy, but Edgardo is already turning into a deer. His stride is drawled and languid, he sweeps the air as he drags his feet, which is how he's been walking in my presence since becoming a teenager, as if every place we go is a tedium, as if he's seen everything a million times before. He talks the same way, too lazy to finish his sentences, to relate, to explain, he's just alive and that's it. Suddenly he'll have a talking spell – it happens about once a month – and he'll spout on for two hours straight, telling me all his adventures at school. But since he's almost lost the ability to express himself, at least with me, his words get all tangled up and he splits his side laughing at the same time he's eating – his fits of grandiloquence usually occur precisely at dinner time; and despite making a staunch effort to concentrate and sharpen my ear, I never under-stand the majority of what he's saying. Then suddenly, once he's repeated each story three times, he looks at me again, as if he suddenly realises that it's his mother he's talking to, calls me stone deaf and shuts hermetically up till the next month's bout. Our other traditional monthly conversation is of the life-is-wonderful variety.

— Do you even realise how lucky we are? Look how beautiful the trees are. Just look at that street. Breathe it in, I tell them during these euphoric instants that seize me every once in a while, thanks to the wine, the kisses, or my own body, whose physical strength and whose last drops of youth are gifts on some days.

Edgar usually looks at me with a long face, Nico pretends to take a deep breath, and he tells me they already know, I've said the same thing a thousand times, today's spectacular street is our same street, the one we walk down four times a day, and what he really wants to do is go to Florence like I promised a few years ago. You always threatened him with not going to Egypt. 'If you don't behave, we won't go to Egypt,' you'd say to him. In the end, the revolution and your disease prevented you from going. The last trip you wanted to take was to Florence. When I told you I couldn't take care of both you and Edgar at the same time, that if you had a turn for the worse while we were so far away, I wouldn't know how to deal with it – in Barcelona, the dance of the ambulances and wheelchairs and late-night trips to the emergency room had already begun – you got so angry with me you told me that I always ruin everything. Marisa wanted to go to Rome and I promised that when she got out of hospital, we would go. We also planned on spending some time at your house where she would teach me how

70

to make her famous gazpacho and legendary croquettes, since she would never be able to return to Cadaqués and live on her own. But it was already too late. I wasn't there when she died suddenly, either. I hadn't been there for two days, completely unaware of how much faster life proceeds inside a hospital, where the wicks burn lickety split, and life and death run crazed races down the aseptic hallways like the cartoon Coyote and the Road Runner, frantic and frenzied, skidding around the nurses and visitors, screwing up our lives. Maybe we all end up with some untaken trip, we plan journeys when they are no longer possible, as if we were trying to buy more time knowing we've used up our own, and that nobody can give us a single minute more. How unbearable to think while our eyes are still open that there are places to which we'll never return, to realise that an opportunity has closed even before our eyes have.

Edgar looks at the three of us petulantly from the top of the stairs and quips: — I'm hungry – can we go now?

Daniel and Nico come up a second later, accompanied by Úrsula, who looks at us and says: — You all look so beautiful!

Sofía is wearing her spectacular floor-length, wine-coloured Indian dress that she bought at an antiquarian. It's dusted with tiny mirrored lozenges, and she set it off with a pair of big silver earrings. I have on my baggy faded fuchsia cotton trousers, a raggedy black silk shirt with little green polka dots, flip-flops, and one of my mother's old bracelets that sometimes I love and sometimes feels more like a shackle. Elisa is dressed as if we were going out to dance salsa. And Úrsula has put on a very tight yellow T-shirt with a silver palm-tree motif and purple jeans about two sizes too small. We look like a troupe of clowns. Fortunately, the children have brought a modicum of summer respectability with their polo shirts, Bermuda shorts and flip-flops.

Carolina and Pep have a small apartment just a little way uphill from our house. It's part of a summer complex that was also built in the seventies, with heavy cement walls painted white and stairways made of reddish wood, long corridors and huge windows that give fabulous views overlooking the town and the bay. When I was young, the apartments had been a sort of hippy colony, where colourful characters from around the world lived. I remember listening to the music and laughter from my bed at night, the din of that group of beautiful summer castaways who I thought were just the most fascinating and exotic people on earth, who returned to Holland, the US or Germany at summer's end. As I got older, so did the hippies, and the apartments began filling with modern people of the nineties, respectable and rich. But those of us who were lucky enough to catch a glimpse through the keyhole of childhood at the tail end of the spirit of the sixties – the sexual freedom, the freedom full stop, the desire to have fun, the empowerment of youth, the sheer audacity – weren't left unscathed. We've all lost some paradise to which we never belonged.

Pep and Hugo are preparing dinner. They've dressed for a summer night. Clean jeans, a perfectly old and faded shirt for Pep and a crisp white shirt with rolled-up sleeves for Hugo. They're both tanned. Hugo likes to run and he wears string bracelets. He smells a little of patchouli and vanilla and he owns some sort of business. Pep is a photographer, his head is shaved and he has a deep voice. Tall and thin, he's the sensitive type, discreet and very funny. You can tell they've been close friends for a long time – they even finish each other's sentences, poke fun at each other, refer to each other as 'bro'. There are no fissures, no doubts; they get together every week to watch football and drink beer. Sometimes I envy this kind of male bonding; seen from the outside it seems like a straighter and more effortless style of friendship than what exists between women. Ours is like an eternal courtship, with its rough patches, intense and passionate, while theirs is more like a well-matched marriage, without strong emotions, maybe, but without boundless ups and downs either.

— So, are we hungry? Pep asks the children.

— Very, Sofía answers, diving into the hummus.

We sit at a table in the garden. Hugo opens the wine and sits down next to me smiling.

— You look beautiful, he says.

— Well, Nico told me I looked like cat food this morning. And children never lie.

— That's an urban myth. Children lie as much as adults do.

— I guess. I lie all the time. And it's not even my worst defect.

We both laugh. He says: — Why don't we go out for dinner sometime, just the two of us? And I try to convince him that I'm a complete mess and that inviting me to dinner isn't worth the effort. The male technique for seduction involves making a fake list of one's own defects (I'm a sale item, don't waste your time on me), it works pretty well, I see, enjoying myself as I eat and play with my mobile phone. I don't lose it all the time any more. The phone became a diabolical object, the messenger of suffering and anguish during your illness and death. You called every night in the wee hours, demanding that I go to your house, to tell me you were afraid, that the home-carer tried to kill you. You might have been partly right. I can't count the number of carers you went through in the last months, but I became an expert at interviewing candidates, most of whom never lasted more than a few days. You didn't allow them a minute's sleep; you'd steal the medication – there were pills scattered all over the house, the floors, in your sheets, in your papers and the pages of your books, I started to fear for the dogs; you fired them two or three times a day, you even punched one of them. What a shame the main character of the story was you. If someone had told us these stories about someone else back in the good old days, we probably would have split our sides laughing. A good laugh was always our best weapon; it's how we dealt with misery and mean-spiritedness. The disease, the pain that some doctors claimed you invented, turned you into a selfish monster. When I told you I couldn't leave the children by themselves at four in the morning, you'd get outraged and hang up on me. Most of our conversations during the last few months ended with you hanging up on me. Every time the phone rang and I saw your number, my heart would skip a beat. Finally I disconnected it, I forgot to charge it, I left it everywhere, I lost it on purpose. Occasionally I'd press answer thinking today she's calling just to tell me she loves me and she's sorry for having abandoned me, and you'd called to talk about money and to reproach me because I was the one who had abandoned you. I did my best, sometimes I did what I had to do, though not always – I'm not very good at facing despair. I'm sorry. Maybe if you'd been in my shoes, you'd have done a better job. For years, you said that you had never loved your mother, that she wasn't a good person, that she'd never loved you. It wasn't until the bitter end that you changed your mind. Those last days in the hospital you mistakenly called me 'Mama' a few times. My grandmother had a very distinguished, silent, elegant and fearless death as befitted her status and character. Yours was total mayhem. Nobody warns you that you have to become your mother when she's dying. And, Mum, you can't say you gave me so much satisfaction as your daughter, either. You yourself weren't an easy daughter.

But since Santi has reappeared, the mobile phone has become something playful again, and we're always just one message away from what can happen next. And what can happen next is almost always more exciting than what is happening now. I like sex because it nails me into the present time. Your death did, too. Not Santi, no, Santi is the same as a mobile. I'm always waiting for something wonderful to come that never does. He was separated from his wife when we met. She was having an affair with a friend of his, but the affair didn't pan out, and Santi, who is a very nice man, went back home with the idea of healing the wounds and mending a relationship that had fallen into the trap of substituting sex, curiosity and admiration for comfort, companionship and children. And our affair, which had already begun to flag a few months in – most love affairs last either a few months or an entire lifetime – was stirred back to life with the thrill of the forbidden, the unattainable, the fantasy. Both of us swallowed the narrative whole. Me because I hadn't found anyone I liked better. Him because he realised right away that the relationship with his wife was going right back into the rut it came from, the last page before closing a book. There is no reverse in a love story; any relationship is always a one-way street.

He texts me that he just got in, he really wants to see me. And so my head once again succumbs to my body, and your death recedes a few more steps into the distance, and as if by magic, my frozen blood begins to flow again. I joke around with the children, I sniff at the food, I lie down on the ground to play with my goddaughter, I hug Sofía, I whisper into Pep's ear that we have a mountain of dope, I pet the cat, I devour olives like a madwoman, I tell everyone to go out and just look at the moon. I put music on and tell Elisa we should go dancing.

— He just texted, I whisper to Sofía.

— I thought so. Your face changed so drastically I knew something was up.

— It's strange. I don't really even like him that much.

— Blanquita, I think you like him that much, you just don't want to admit it.

— Maybe I do, I don't know.

We have dinner in the garden outside. The candles are lit and there are a few Chinese lanterns swaying from the branches of the olive tree. Their shadows sway over the pristine crust of salt-cooked fish the men have prepared; there's tomato and cucumber salad and croquettes, and recently baked olive bread. Children and adults alike are tanned and happy, the relaxed, tired bodies and dreamy eyes of a day spent boating, in the sea and the sun. We share stories, the same ones repeated a thousand times by people who have spent large portions of their lives together and still like each other. For a fleeting moment, I consider having a quiet coffee and not responding to the message. Nina, my goddaughter, is sleeping in her mother's lap. Edgar is trying to sneak a little swig of beer, but he stops when Elisa looks at him threateningly. Nico is paying attention to the adults' conversation while little Dani is playing with his collection of trains. Hugo accuses me of being a bore. Carolina comes out in my defence and Pep starts telling stories of Hugo's poor girlfriends, left behind every morning while he goes out for his sacred run. I can't imagine life having any meaning without these summer nights. I get another text from Santi and he proposes that we meet up in front of the church to give me a goodnight kiss. I get up, as if I had been sitting on a spring.

— I have to go out for a minute – be right back.

Everyone looks at me with surprise.

— Anything wrong, dear? Are you OK? Carolina asks with a worried expression.

— Yes, I'm fine. I'm just going out to buy cigarettes, I say with a giggle.

— Yeah, Sofía says.

Carolina looks at me from the other side of the table without smiling. She's the only one of us who has had a long-term relationship with a really wonderful man, and though she's never expressed it, I know she considers my dating a married man not only a waste of time but also in some way a bit of a betrayal of her, too.

Hugo picks up and wiggles a half-full pack of cigarettes at me, which he had put out on the table a little while ago.

— That tobacco's stale. Seriously, it's totally unsmokable, I say.

He laughs. — When you told me you fib a lot, I imagined you'd be a little better at it.

— I do what I can.

— Don't take too long, we'll be bored without you, he adds.

Sofía accompanies me to the door.

— You don't really like him that much, huh?

9

I skip down the hill with a spring in my step. You always said I walked like my father, as if there were something pushing me upwards, as if our feet barely grazed the ground, and how before seeing us you already knew we were coming by the unmistakable pattern of our gait. I still recall how angry you got that one time when I was near the end of my pregnancy and you saw me lumbering.

'Please don't tell me you're going to change the way you've walked your entire life, just because you're pregnant.'

If you were to see me now, you'd know perfectly well that I'm on my way to meet a man. But you never tried to stop me. You believed that love justified the type of quirky behaviour that under normal circumstances you would have roundly disapproved of. If a waiter brought you the wrong dish, or spilled soup on you, and in response to your complaint the maître d' would say that it's on account of his being in love – you alone were able to squeeze these kinds of intimate details from others – you would have looked at him with a kind face and said, 'Oh, well, in that case . . .' And go back to eating, happy as a clam, with a soup stain on your skirt. But if someone dared give you information assuring you it was right and it turned out to be wrong, or showed up late for a meeting, you'd stare at them as if stupefied, and they'd lose your respect forever. I spent my entire life fighting to gain that respect without ever knowing whether I succeeded. I still run late, no matter where I go.

Unexpectedly, I find the beautiful stranger approaching me in long strides. He's alone, walking a little hunched forward, like most tall, reedy men do, as if protecting themselves from invisible gusts of wind, as if it were always a little blustery up there in the air they inhabit. I'm walking so fast and feeling so restless that one of my flip-flops accidentally falls off. I recover it just in time to see that he's caught me in the act, which elicits a teasing smile. Again, just wave goodbye to the femme fatale I've always aspired to be. I smile back at him as we pass by each other, and he whispers: — Later, Cinderella. I think, what if I stop and suggest having a drink (and we get drunk together and spill our life stories to each other eagerly and in little episodes while we stroke each other's hands and pinch each other's knees dreamily, and look searchingly into each other's eyes a split second longer than is appropriate, and then we kiss, and then we fuck impetuously in some corner of the town like when we were young, and fall in love and travel together and be forever spooning each other and we have a few more children and, yes, in the end we save each other), but I continue walking and don't look back. If men only knew how many times women play that film over in their heads, they'd never dare ask us for a light.

Santi is sitting in front of the church door. I'm so happy to see him that I don't even notice how much skinnier he is than the last time we saw each other, or how tired he looks and that he's smoking joints again. He looks at me with a twinkle in his eyes and flashes an ear-to-ear grin.

— You're so brown.

— I'm brown, he responds. — How are you?

— Fine.

We remain quiet for a few seconds, just looking at each other, grinning, suddenly a little shy and speechless, as if the mere fact of being opposite each other again was the most extraordinary thing in the world.

— And the children?

— Fine. They're just happy to be here.

— Do they miss their grandmother?

— I guess. They adored her, they always had such a great time with her, but they aren't really talking about it. They're well mannered, very discreet.

— Like their mother.

— How are yours? Are they well?

— Happy. You should see how well the older one swims, it's amazing. Lately I feel as though I spend the whole day yelling at them.

— Oh dear. How old is the older one? Ten?

— Nine.

— Ah.

— You look so beautiful.

— Thanks. You too. Do you have a cigarette?

He brushes my hand when he brings the lighter up close. And with that gesture we walk off the playground, peel away the thin, awkward, lovesick skin of teenagers and return to being two foolish adults with worn-out skin in a long-term illicit relationship.

— I don't have much time. I told them I needed to buy cigarettes. I just wanted to see you, Blanca. Know how you're doing. But I have to leave pretty soon.

— You have time for a drink, don't you?

— No. I wish I did. They've organised a huge barbecue on the beach and they're going to notice I'm not there.

He pretends not to see the disappointment in my eyes.

— When will we see each other again?

— I'm not sure. One of these days.

— You're such an arsehole.

— Did I already tell you how beautiful you are tonight?

I smoke in silence. He grabs my trousers and pulls them up to my waist. Then he twirls me around as if I were a puppet to look at my arse.

— Will I ever be able to get you to wear trousers that fit?

— Doubt it.

— How about leggings? You'd look awesome.

— Sure.

— Leather ones.

We both chuckle at the idea.

— I'll buy a pair tomorrow.

He kisses me, still holding me by the trousers.

— I don't want you to be angry with me. Get it? I can't stand it when you're angry. It makes me feel really bad.

I giggle. — Yeah, so, so bad.

— Go ahead, laugh, laugh at me. But it's true.

— Well, I'm not angry, I say. But mentally, I have already begun counting the minutes until he's gone and I'll be left alone and your death will come back to haunt me and everything will start all over again. For all the love of my friends, of my children, it isn't enough to withstand the impact of your not being here – I need to be held tightly by a man so as not to fly away. They say that most women look for their father in other men, but I look for you, I did even when you were alive. Any dishonest psychiatrist would have a field day with me, and yet mine only wants me to find a job.

— What are you thinking about? One minute you're here and the next you're off somewhere else.

— I'm thinking about how tired I am.

— Tired of what?

— I don't know. Everything. The day. The summer, which is very tiring. I think I need to sleep.

— Do you realise we've never slept together? Well, maybe once, right at the beginning. I made breakfast for you in the morning.

— No, I don't recall that. But I'd love to sleep with you. Sleep-sleep, I mean.

— But there might be nocturnal violation.

— Except it wouldn't be a violation.

He says goodbye and, as usual, without making any specific plans. I stay put for a while, seated in front of the church. I hear the rumour of people in the town out partying, in full summer swing, and ask myself who rules in La Frontera these days, what clan of stoned lunatics goes out to watch the sun rise at Cap de Creus, and whether they still play 'Should I Stay or Should I Go' as the last song of the night in El Hostal before closing. The first crown a person loses, and perhaps the only one that can never be regained is that of youth: childhood doesn't count because we're not even aware yet of the incredible bounty of energy, strength, beauty, freedom and candour that will belong to us in a few years, which the luckiest among us will squander beyond measure.

When I get home, everyone's already in bed. I sneak into Sofía and little Dani's room, the one with the bunk beds. All summer residences are a little like a holiday camp: a big wooden table around which we all meet for breakfast as we wake up, the joy of getting together with friends from early in the morning, dressed in one's pyjamas or swimsuit, bleary-eyed, hung-over or radiant, laughing at the antics of the day before, preparing hot chocolate for the children and arguing over whether it's too early to drink a beer or not, taking turns for the shower, the shrieks of the last person in, who has it cold because there's no warm water left, the line of discoloured towels, stiff from the salt water and drying in the sun, the rooms with the bunk beds to maximise space and fit as many friends in as possible. I climb into bed with Sofía.

— I'm not sleepy, I whisper in her ear.

— Huh? What? What's going on? Dani! and she gives me a little smack.

— No, no, it's me. I just got back.

— How'd it go? she asks, taking off the pink satin eye mask and sitting up a little.

— Fine, fine. Same old thing. We chatted for a while and then he had to leave.

— I see.

— And now I can't sleep.

— I can imagine. It's normal. Since you couldn't fuck. Unresolved sex has a way of keeping a person awake. But it took me an hour to get Daniel to sleep, I haven't been out snogging, and I am pooped.

Dani stirs in his bed.

— If you wake him up, I'll kill you, she whispers.

— Where's your summer spirit?

— Sleeping, she answers, putting her eye mask back on.

I stay there for a while, hoping she'll remember that I'm a poor orphan who needs someone to pay attention to her, but after a few minutes Dani stops moving around and she begins snoring softly.

I go back to my own room. I wonder what the mysterious stranger is doing now. Maybe the same as I am.

10

I wake up the next morning to the sound of a dog barking. I linger curled up in bed thinking it's coming from the street downstairs, maybe it's Rey, I muse, coming to find me. Once, we had as many as five dogs in the house at the same time, three of our own, the one kept by the housecleaner, which was one of the dogs you picked up and saved and then bankrolled for the rest of his life – I remember how you'd carry a collar and lead in your purse, just in case you came across some stray dog – and the fifth belonged to a friend who was staying with us for a bit. You so enjoyed that pack of untouchables; they were like a parallel court to the one of your friends. If any visitor dared to complain or turn away from the dogs' rambunctious charges, or worse, said they were afraid of them, he or she would be reckoned la-di-da, a total pinhead, and never invited back. Unless, that is, their skill as a poker player earned back your respect. I remember a very dapper lady who used to come to play poker. You always placed an immaculate and perfectly folded towel on the back of her chair so she could cover her legs and protect them from the rubbing, licking and dubious hygiene of your dogs.

I hear Guillem's booming voice. He's just arrived with Patum. I can already tell it's going to be a beautiful day before opening the curtains, just from the way the light is filtering through the fabric. I'll go to the cemetery to visit you today. I put on one of the crumpled silk dresses that are tangled together with the rest of my clothes in a precarious bunch on the only chair in the room. I don't even enjoy buying clothes any more, which used to be my main hobby. Despite the heat, the only clothes I buy now are the kind that cover me up or that hug me. In any case, clothes are nothing more than a substitute for sex, or at least a means for getting it. Maybe everything is a substitute for sex: food, money, the sea, power, even sex itself. I open the curtain and let the summer sunshine in, so young and brazen, so exactly as it was in my childhood, and it spills across the room.

Guillem shows up loaded with boxes of vegetables.

— Quick, Úrsula, hide them before Blanca has the chance to throw them in the bin! I know her too well, he says when he sees me.

— How great that you've come! I say, giving him a hug.

— Yeah, now you have another person to torture, eh?

I'm glad to see him. He's definitely a person who

would not send me to a nursing home. I used to measure how much I could trust a person by asking myself whether they would have been a collaborator in occupied France, but now my trial by fire is whether they would send me to a nursing home. Or to the stake for being a witch. You always said in that peculiar way of yours, as if insulting me and praising me all at the same time, that I wouldn't have lasted five minutes in the Middle Ages.

The children are upstairs, having breakfast in front of the television.

— You mean to tell me they're watching television at this time of the morning, and on a day like this? Guillem cries.

Úrsula is freshly showered, her hair and skin aglow, and she's wearing one of her very skinny tops with a tropical motif. She laughs and sips her coffee quietly. The good thing about Úrsula for people like me who don't like having help is that, with her, it's almost the same as not having any. Elisa appears through the kitchen door with cups, saucers and toast, followed by Damián. I haven't seen her alone once since we arrived in Cadaqués.

— Morning, lovely, how are you feeling? she says by way of a greeting.

Her stunning shock of hair is loose and she has a white sundress on, very red toenails, and her silver sandals have been accessorised with an ankle bracelet made of tiny bells. I see we're still in Cuban mode, I think facetiously. Elisa likes clothes and every time she changes her boyfriend, she changes her style.

— There are days, though, when what I really want to do is go out completely nude, she told me once with the trademark candour of a gorgeous, uninhibited woman who knows that beauty is its own dress, so she's never truly naked.

Damián is wearing grey jeans cut off at the knee, an old shirt, navy-blue trainers with matching socks, and a fabulous bangle he always wears at his wrist, made of bronze and turquoise. I tried to take it from him several times, but he says he can't get it off. He put it on when he was a teenager, before leaving Cuba. And when he tried to take it off later on – when he broke up with the girlfriend who had given it to him – he'd grown so much that he could no longer slip the bracelet over his hand. I met Damián years before I met Elisa, through a mutual friend at the launch of an anthology of young Cuban poets. He's restrained, kind, affectionate and fun-loving; he likes women, alcohol and drugs, but I've never seen him flaunting any one of the three. I think he's a good man, although it's hard to tell with people until you need a favour, or when it comes to taking sides, which always happens sooner or later. At least he looks you in the eye, he's always the same person no matter who he's with, and I've never heard him say a bad word about anyone. He likes to laugh more than talk, and when he does talk it's to divulge some complicated socio-political theory that nobody really understands anyway. I wouldn't be surprised if he were one of those people who think the first moon-walking mission was a hoax. He's tall and thin, but fluffy and rounded at the same time, his features are lazy like hills, there's nothing sharp to them like the style of men I prefer, nothing perverse, aquiline or defeated in him, no hidden storms on the horizon, and the sky one touches by his side probably doesn't reach beyond the ceiling, the bedroom ceiling that is. But of course Elisa sees him as a sort of Greek god type, a dangerous predator, a Don Juan who has had affairs with half the city. When you fall in love – she insists she's not, that he's just a lover and nothing more, a strong sign that she probably is – the way you think about your object of desire never corres-ponds with reality, especially with regards to physical allure. How good it would be if we could only preserve this truth for the next time round, but love always returns the settings back to zero, and if we're lucky, the next man that comes along will once again be the most handsome, sexy, smart, fun and amazing man in the world, even though he's really a halfwit hunchback.

Sofía bursts through the door, dragging Dani with her. She's just back from town and has a bottle of champagne in hand. She's wearing a truly bizarre straw hat with a black bow that looks like an upside-down ice-cream cone with the tip cut off, huge bug-eye sunglasses, and a black dress tied at the neck, which showcases her delicate collar-bone and shoulders.

— Look what I found in town!

She stares at Guillem for a few seconds and I watch as surprise, curiosity, interest and glee all pass hurriedly across her countenance one by one.

— Oh, champagne, he says sarcastically. — Wouldn't a bottle of whisky have been more appropriate? Champagne is for those silly chichi types. What do you think, Úrsula?

— I don't know, Mr Guillem, I don't drink.

— Yeah, right, he responds. In this house you have to mark the level of liquid in the bottles before going to bed.

— I had to buy it. I just received terrible news. My gynaecologist died.

— Oh, I'm so sorry, I say. — That's terrible.

She sits at the table looking downcast and quiet, lost in thought. I had no idea she was so fond of her gynaecologist. I wonder briefly if she's going to steal the wind from my grief.

— Don't you get it? she exclaims abruptly, raising her head. — He's the first man to die who's had his hands in my cunt.

I breathe a sigh of relief.

— We're getting so old, Elisa sighs philosophically.

— I'm fabulous, Sofía says. Better than ever.

— Come on, Posh, pass the bottle over and I'll put it in the fridge to chill, Guillem says. — We can see how upset you are.

— What did he call me? Sofía asks, opening her eyes widely.

— Posh, you know, the Spice Girl who's a little chichi, I say.

Sofía snorts daintily. —That's odd. I'm not the least bit chichi.

— What's odd is the hat you're wearing, Guillem says.

— Well. Who wants to go boating? Boys! Get ready. We leave in twenty minutes. Posh, go and put your swim-suit on.

There was nothing in the world you liked more than to go out on the boat. I'll look for one of the photos of you at the helm of *Tururut* as soon as I gather the courage to open the photo albums you gave me on my last birthday, a few months before you died – I told you I wasn't inter-ested in your precious figurines or valuable books and paintings, the only thing I wanted was the family photo albums my grandfather had started and you continued, and then you showed up with a huge purple suitcase full of them, dragging it along with great difficulty and the help of a carer. They're an irrefutable testament that we had been happy. A photo where you're smiling; your hair is wind-blown and salty, and I'll place it with the rest of the photos on the shelf, next to Papa's. I haven't done it so far, because you aren't a memory yet. I imagine that time, the bastard, the all-merciful, will see to that.

Guillem is wearing an old captain's hat he dug out of a box in the garage and leads the small force down the cobblestone streets and onwards to the pier, passing muster before the unflappable gaze of the church, gleaming in the sunlight. Houses are assembled around it like an army of obedient soldiers, forming a compact and harmonious mass only broken here and there by the vibrant fuchsia of a bougainvillea or the weathered green of a random tree. The mountains rise up behind the town, once covered in olive trees, isolating it from the rest of the region and practically turning it into an island. The sea, tame or angry, gloomy or euphoric, wicked or coy, is speckled with tired, empty boats, and seems to be paying homage to a place that neither time nor the hordes of tourists have been able to ruin.

The children wait dutifully on the pier next to Guillem and Patum for the boatman to come and transport us out to our wharf, dressed in orange life jackets that echo the colour of the buoys bobbing on the water's surface. Hugo and Pep talk softly between themselves, Carolina tries to stop little Nina from jumping into the water, and we go for a beer run.

Guillem immediately befriends the boatman, who gives his phone number for when we're ready to come back in.

— Posh, remind me to buy him a bottle of rum when we're in town this afternoon, would you?

The sea is like a silver plate; its surface sparkles as if all the stars of the night before had fallen in. I reach into the water and let my hand drag against the movement, feel the current between my fingers, the three foamy columns that leave a wake behind and disappear almost instantly. At the bottom I glimpse tiny grey fish stirring like little ghosts. Then the beach and its human rainbow, the sounds of laughter, the shouting and splashing all dissipate into the distance, as we move full speed ahead. When we get to our boat, Guillem asks us to board in an orderly fashion and tells us where to sit. Afterwards, and with Edgar's help, he pulls the tiller and rudder blade out and plants himself smack in the middle. He adjusts his captain's hat and starts to imitate you.

— All right then, children, don't anyone move from their spot, a boat can be a very dangerous place. Edgar, Edgar, put the tiller in its place. Careful now! Careful there, don't fall in! Wait, where's that anchor? Oh, it's in the water! Let's just hope we haven't snagged it in the rocks. Who's going to jump in to unsnag the anchor? No, it's not? Oh, thank goodness. The keys! Where are the keys? Whose job was it to bring the keys? My bag! My bag! Where is it? The glasses! The glasses! Don't anyone move!

It's such a perfect imitation that we roar with laughter.

Then he sucks the tip of his index finger, raises it high and frowns with his eyebrows knitted looking out over the horizon, and turns into Paco, one of your best friends.

— Let's see if today the Garbi doesn't just kick up. Ohhh, yes. The situation is tricky, could get critical at some point. Might be better to stay close, a quick swim and back home in a jiffy.

— But the sea is calm, there's not a single drop of wind, Nico complains.

94

— Look, kid, I've been sailing my entire life. I know what I'm talking about. If you don't want to listen, I'm jumping ship. You can figure it out yourselves. And when you're dragged out to Mallorca by the current, just remember I told you so. 'Cause when I was a boy . . .

The boat glides smoothly across the water, the motor's raspy, old smoker's rattle prevents conversation, but for the time being there's no need for words, our attention is distracted, we stare out into the distance; the best thing about beauty is that it often comes with silence and obliges people to collect themselves. I feel Nico's warm, plump little hand in mine. The boys, guided by Guillem, take turns at the tiller. Edgar is sitting straddled at the bow, the way I used to sit when I was his age, and Sofía is sipping a beer with her eyes closed. Patum is sleeping, stretched out at my feet. Pep is taking photos, obliged by his profession to keep an eye open. Carolina holds a drowsy Nina, lulled by the sound of the motor, in her lap and Hugo is lying back in the sun. We anchor in a small cove where there are only two other boats whose occupants greet us politely. The water is so transparent it looks as if we could touch the jagged, menacing rocks at the bottom with our feet, but it's really about twenty metres deep. As soon as the motor's drilling stops, we all rouse from our daydream state as if a hypnotist had snapped her fingers. Patum is an expert swimmer, in keeping with her race, and starts barking and springing about excitedly. Edgar is the first one to dive in; Patum is right behind him and he almost lands on his head. The little ones prepare to walk down the ladder while Guillem, with Hugo's help, assures that the boat is well anchored.

— Oh dear, Sofía exclaims suddenly. — I just realised something. I forgot my swimsuit! She looks at us like a naughty little girl.

The boys keep to their tasks, pretending they haven't heard what she said. Hugo raises an eyebrow under his sunglasses and smiles imperceptibly, though he remains horizontal and doesn't move. Guillem looks at her sideways and continues testing the anchor's line, perhaps tugging at it just a tad sharper than a minute ago. Pep, without removing his eye from the camera's objective, deviates the lens modestly out towards the sea. And Nico, who's been wearing his swimming trunks from the moment he jumped out of bed this morning, whispers in my ear:

— Sofía's a little dippy, isn't she? How could she forget her swimsuit?

— I see. It took you half an hour to change, you kept us waiting in the car, dying of heatstroke like sardines in a tin can, and you forgot your swimsuit, I say, looking at her playfully.

— Exactly. I'm so clueless!

— Yeah.

— Well, skinny-dip then, Carolina says, — it's more pleasant, anyway.

And with the same natural elegance as when she slips out of a fur stole in winter – or when she falls asleep on the sofa, or in the middle of the lawn when the alcohol closes her eyes and she's already told me a thousand times how much she loves me – she lets the ankle-length pink-and-grey-striped tunic slide from her shoulders. She dives into the water head first, and her body, like a caramel-coloured ray of light, submerges with the grace and precision of a professional swimmer, silently and without a splash.

— Maybe her gynaecologist was one of the few to have had his hands in it, and a few other poor wretches, but we've all had the pleasure of seeing it now, haven't we? Carolina sighs.

I settle onto the ladder to get used to the water slowly. I hate the shock of cold water, it makes me bristle and infuriates me, making all the muscles of my body go tense. Finally I let go, and allow the water's cold blade graze me, eyes closed, hair like a jelly fish dancing atop my submerged head. I'm weightless at last, I feel welcome, blessed, and absolved. I wonder if the sea will be my last lover.

11

I'm the first one into the shower, and when I'm finished I go up to the kitchen to serve myself a glass of chilled white wine and stretch out in the hammock on the terrace until lunch is ready. That's when Elisa approaches, frowning.

— We don't have enough food for lunch, she says.

— Oh, that's too bad, I answer. — Well, there are biscuits, aren't there?

— It's not a joke.

I intuit that my half-hour break, my white wine and privileged spot on the hammock are in danger. — It's scorching and I'm tired. You can't expect me to go shopping now, I say, closing my eyes and rocking a little harder.

— Yes, I can. She's quiet for a minute, waiting for me to open my eyes, but I am a truly lazy being, and so I don't. But she, who is truly stubborn, holds out. — Blanquita, I've just spent half the morning cleaning and cooking, so get up this very instant and go buy some sausages, she says commandingly, interrupting the swing of my hammock.

I put up a weak fight, and threaten that I'm going to pass out on the way, and hit my head against a rock, and when I bleed to death it'll be her fault, but she doesn't budge.

— Oh, all riiiiiight. I'll go. But I just really don't get this bourgeois need to eat lunch and then dinner. You're all so fickle, anyway.

The sea is like a huge magnet; it empties the town of people, drags the majority of them to the shore. Only a few castaways meander along the sleepy streets looking for the shade of houses devastated by the sun. You have to reach a certain age before it's possible to feel affection for the city you were born in, or where you spent your childhood, before you stop allowing familiarity to keep your eyes closed, or stop wanting to run away to find a new adventure every morning. I like Barcelona because it's where my life has happened – this is the hospital where Edgar was born, this bar is where I clandestinely kissed his father, here I would have an afternoon snack with my grandfather every Wednesday, and this is where you died. But I think I'd have fallen in love with Cadaqués even if I had only stopped by one afternoon on my way somewhere else, even if I were from the other side of the world and shared no cultural baggage, no language, no memories, nothing else that tied me to the steep, craggy landscape and its cul-de-sac shoreline where the silky pink sunsets are whipped by a black wind to fade over the sea, where everything pushes you out towards the clouds and the sky.

I walk into the butcher's and feel relieved by the cold slap of air conditioning. I'd never before realised how closely a butcher's shop resembles a hospital, and the thought gives me goosebumps as I take in the greyish-white colour of the walls and floor, the row of empty chairs where ladies usually sit and wait their turn, the knives like surgical instruments prepared for cutting, and the track of fluorescent tubes across the ceiling with their icy, unflattering light. I hope I don't run into a boyfriend because I must look awful. Once again, I'd become a terrible disappointment. I notice there's a woman who has her back turned to me, in front of the refrigerated display case with strings of sausage links, mountains of meat, and rows of fresh offal, tender and juicy: it's Santi's wife. We've never been introduced, but I've seen photos of her and her children in Santi's house, and undoubtedly she knows what I look like too. I feel a blend of excitement and panic, and a little pang of distaste, though I'm fully aware that she's the only one of us who has a right to that emotion. She's younger than I am, with a solid, pleasing physique. Her neck is short and thick, and she has a wide, bulky torso that's set atop thin legs, a round face and chestnut-coloured eyes, very large and a little vacant. She's tanned, and her hair is combed back into a ponytail. She's wearing a long, flowing turquoise wrap with a matching beaded necklace. Despite her short stature and realist, earth-bound exterior, she speaks to the butcher in a high-pitched voice and without looking at him, showing the typical sense of superiority and condescending gregariousness of the rich. I feel terribly uncomfortable, as if I were shrinking with every minute that passed, as if her voice of command and control and her contained impatience were directed at me. All of a sudden she turns round. And her heavy-lidded glance slips right past without seeing me. She doesn't look surprised, or indignant, there's no curiosity or even the slightest shudder of encountering another living thing, she simply doesn't see me. She grabs her bags and exits with a muffled goodbye. I breathe a sigh of relief and incredulity – I could never be in a place without instantly stopping and registering everything and everyone around me – and immediately begin fantasising about what might have happened. I'm truly happy it didn't happen, that there was no drama of humiliated, furious and scornful official wife, versus cruel, pathetic and digni-fied lover played out over a background of cold cuts and sausages. It makes me feel a little sorry for Santi, who has chosen to sleep next to this attractive yet authoritarian woman to the very end of his days.

I leave the butcher shop sausage-laden and make a quick stop at the casino to buy cigarettes and have a draught beer. I discover my mystery man sitting in the penumbra at a table in the back, where the town's old men usually sit and play cards. For a second I childishly think you must have placed him there for me as some sort of a sign. You were so worried that I hadn't fallen in true love for such a long time, turning what you thought so important into a game that I was playing with opponents who you considered – in typical mum fashion – below my skill set and not on my level. You said: 'Little one, at your age, you're supposed to be in love. I don't understand what you're doing.' For a long time, the only love story I cared about was ours.

I sit down at the table next to his. He smiles openly, as if we already knew each other.

— Lose any shoes today? he asks, leaning forward and looking at my feet.

We both laugh. He has a thoughtful, relentless, sensitive look in his eyes, a little sad, that he turns away occasionally out of shyness. His large mouth has kiss-me lips that are masculine but soft enough to nibble, and it curves a little when he laughs, adding a boyish look to his otherwise formidable Greek-hero head. His bushy eyebrows are darker than the burnished gold of his thick, cropped hair. The colour must get darker in the winter and it sits like a crown, or a frothy cloud, atop a slightly bulging forehead. His prominent chin is covered in a four-day beard that probably only took him two to grow. His almond-shaped eyes are wide-set, dark grey and stormy, as if they want to invade the space of his temples so as not to miss anything going on around him. His voice is deep and rich but unaffected; it neither denies nor confirms his appearance.

— Not yet, I say. — It's easy to lose a flip-flop when you're walking fast because there's no grip. You know? I tell him, gesticulating and moving my foot so he can see how the shoe moves. And how thin and delicate my ankle is.

— Yeah. I only wear espadrilles. In the summer, I mean. I'm not very into fashion.

— No, I'm not either. There I go telling fibs already, I think. In another minute I'll be telling him how passionate I am about football, and that the only thing I read is poetry.

— Aren't you going to the beach?

— We just got back. My skin is delicate, I can't be in the sun during these hours of the day. Well, not ever. According to my dermatologist, my skin is an aberration for this country.

— Yeah. You have a lot of freckles. You're like a map.

I hated them when I was little, nobody ever had freckles like me in school, I was the strange one. Then I got accustomed to them. — And I think, it started when men like you began telling me how much they love them.

— I love freckles.

I flash a grateful smile. I've been lucky; I've never underestimated or taken for granted men's affection, I know how much my life depends on it.

— Has anyone ever counted them before?

— No . . .

— I imagine you'd lose count along the way.

We both have a good laugh.

— More or less.

— I'm good with numbers. And he looks away, frowning, as if suddenly he had to pay attention to some important and complicated subject.

— I'm certain you are. Can I ask you something?

— Sure, go ahead.

— What were you doing at my mother's funeral? That was you, wasn't it?

— Yeah, it was me.

— Did you know her?

— No, my father did.

— Don't tell me we're siblings.

He laughs again. — No, not that I know of.

— Oh, thank God.

— When my father was young, he had a little place for live music, very low-key, more like a den. Your mother was a regular. My father used to play the guitar and sing after hours and there was a song she always used to ask him to sing, it was her favourite.

He talks as if he were telling me a story, once upon a time, a long time ago, as if he had a box of marvellous pearls and for some mysterious reason he had decided to give them all to me. I pull my chair up closer to his.

— Which song?

— I don't remember, it must have been some Argentine song. And he continues. — My father was obviously fascinated with the woman, so cultivated and modest, shy and amiable, who came from uptown and who was thrilled to hear his songs.

— I've never heard this story.

— You probably weren't even born yet. One day, after the show, my father mentioned that he was having money problems. They weren't friends, but they chatted from time to time, like regulars in a bar tend to do. Your mother told him to meet her in her office the next day. When he got there, she asked how much money he needed, then opened a drawer and gave it to him. Without asking when he could give it back, or what he needed it for, without asking for any kind of guarantee, hardly knowing him. She simply opened the drawer and gave him the money. My father returned every last cent, but never forgot that gesture of kindness.

— What happened next? Did they see each other again? Where's your father?

— Nothing happened. He must have needed the money to pay off some debts – my father was a disaster as a businessman. The bar ended up closing and my father went back to Argentina. He died a few years ago. I was born here – my mother is Catalan. When I found out that your mother had died and she would be buried in Cadaqués, I decided to show up and pay my respects and thank her on behalf of my father.

— Why didn't you approach me?

— I didn't think it was the right time. You had a lot of people around.

— You would have made my day.

He laughs again, looking in the distance. — You think?

— Maybe not. I guess the day was pretty much ruined no matter what. Who was the girl by your side?

— A friend. That's what friends are for, right? To go on a bender with, to be with you at funerals, those types of things.

The phone rings suddenly. It's Oscar, he just arrived. They're waiting for me to bring the sausages home.

— I have to run. Ex-husband number two just got in.

He looks shocked. — How many of them are there?

I laugh. — That's it, that's it, only two. The normal amount for someone my age with itchy feet.

— Ah. Well, see you around.

I run out of the bar while I play with the pink pearls I now have in my pocket, soft and warm.

12

The big redwood table with its iron foot the colour of lapis lazuli takes up the entire dining room. My uncle designed it. There's a small wood-framed hatch that connects this space to the tiny kitchen so the dishes can be passed straight through without having to get up. It was designed when there were no children and everyone usually dined out. The windows and doors were arranged strategically, to keep the air circulating, and the room swathed in gauzy light, with no shadows. Oscar and Guillem treat each other respectfully and behave graciously, and treat the other one's son with something close to paternal love. I'm not sure how we got here; we're each so impassioned and manic in our own way, so allergic to the gratuitous promiscuity and soft tolerance that's so characteristic of our generation. Oscar jokes with Edgar about the little fuzz on his lip, while Guillem ties Nico's napkin around his neck so he doesn't soil his shirt. Sofía flirts with Guillem, who disagrees with her on everything, poking fun at what she says, which is also one of the oldest forms of seduction in the book. Elisa and Damián whisper secrets to each other, plunged into their stormy world of besotted lovers. She rolls joints for him. Her hands work fast and determinedly, using precise movements that are feminine, almost maternal, with her head cocked to one side as if she were sewing, a soft curtain of hair covering her face. When she's finished, she places them delicately in front of the plate like an offering. Suddenly, it seems as though I were witnessing a voluntary act of submission, and there's something slightly erotic and improper about it, the type of things that should only happen in the bedroom and in private; a form of service, an act much more intimate than swimming in the nude. You brought me up so fervently and effectively against any form of submission that isn't for fun or something playful, that I never had any need to become a feminist.

Guillem bought two kilos of mussels, and we devour them as if we haven't had enough of the sea yet. We drink chilled white wine as if it were water. Elisa silently disapproves of our greedy, selfish way of eating, which is exacerbated by the time spent outdoors and on the boat – more than once she's been left without meat or salad or cake because she was in the kitchen preparing something. I regard my children's metamorphosis from city princes to golden, salty-skinned little barbarians. Every once in a while when I catch him looking the other way, I take a lick of Nico's chubby little cheek that's peppered with freckles. He pretends to get angry and tries to get me back, only to end up dying of laughter. At our best of times, we're just like a pride of lions.

Sofía explains to Oscar for the umpteenth time that she manages an important business.

— How can a crazy goat like her have a job like that? he whispers. — Or is she just making it up so we think she's interesting?

And his majestic bull's head, with its deep, symmetrically square jaw and strong, thoughtful forehead, belts out a laugh that sounds like a mischievous child, the way so many men's laughter does. Just like the children, and like Guillem, whose worn, determined hands have something poignant about them, and look a lot like Oscar's. And his soft, dark eyes suddenly fade into those of Santi's, a little more timid, and crazed, and then again they transform into the clearer, more sorrowful eyes of the mysterious stranger I met a while ago, moving like parts of a magical kaleidoscope capable of summoning the fragments of the past, the present and the future.

We don't have to say anything. As soon as we see each other, even if it's only to have lunch or go to the pharmacy, we immediately turn into a couple again, as if the sum of the parts couldn't be found anywhere else, as if we were the exact and perfect formula for something, even though we've never succeeded, and maybe never will, in figuring out exactly what.

— Why aren't we together again?

The sun filters in through the faded pink of the curtains, bathing the entire room in a warm, golden radiance with glimmers of red. I feel the silly and irresponsible happiness of waking up after a night adrift in kisses and nibbles. Oscar opens an eye and sniggers at me. I remember one of the first times we slept together – he left early to go to work and texted me a little while later: 'I like opening an eye and seeing you by my side.' We jumped head first into the maelstrom that turns mere mortals into invincible gods and makes them think they're not alone. When my relationship with Guillem ended, I thought it meant I would be exiled from that territory forever, and here I was back again for a while, with the same certainty and euphoria and blindness and appreciation as the first time. One of the most amazing things about love is how miraculously it rekindles. I haven't set foot on that island whose secret location is lost to us all until the day we open our eyes and there it is again, like magic, we're back.

— Come here.

— No, seriously.

Morning sex takes the energy away that I've accrued while sleeping and turns me into a willowy convalescent for the rest of the day, as if I didn't have any bones. And today I want to visit you in the cemetery.

— Come here, check it out. He raises the sheet with a sheepish grin and shows me his awakening.

But I don't want to jump back into that sea, I need to touch the earth, the gnarled olive trees, feel burning stones, watch the high, anaemic clouds.

— Seriously, Oscar, I want to be your girlfriend, I repeat in a tone that sounds sort of like a girl trying to convince her nanny to buy an ice-cream cone, or let her see a film meant for adults. It's a catty blend of plea and command.

— Blanquita, there's nothing I would like better, you know that, but after a few days you'll send me to hell again.

— No, no. I shake my head vehemently, trying to sweep away all doubts with my straw-like strands of hair. — I won't fuck anyone else but you.

Every time we're together, my body screams out that I'm made for this man, and I still don't heed its irrefutable evidence. Somehow life always gets in the way, insists on negating that evidence with equal and opposite vehemence.

— That's not enough. It's not bad – he looks at me grinning like a wolf, — but it's not enough. You know that. He suddenly looks tired, like an actor who's been playing the same part for years against a much younger and less experienced character.

— But it's a lot, I say, remembering with a slight shudder last night's feelings of wonder and plenitude. — We're still attracted to each other after so many years – that's a lot.

— Yeah, it's amazing. I smile. Give in. Go ahead, give in to the flattery like everyone else, and to the golden light bathing the room, and to his round and slippery shoulders and your own vigorous and supple teenage body, incapable of rejecting anything sensual that's not harmful.

— As soon as I see you my mind says: 'Fuck, fuck, fuck.'

— And we love each other.

— Yes, we do love each other a lot. He's quiet for a minute. — But we can't stand each other. You can't stand me. And you drive me nuts. I've never lost it so entirely as I have with you.

I laugh, although it's been many years since I considered the ability to infuriate my significant other as something of merit, or one of the lowest rungs on the ladder of passion.

— Do you remember that time on the motorcycle when you got so angry – I don't remember why – and you made me get off and you left me standing there in the middle of the street?

— And you threw the helmet at my head and almost caused an accident?

— Let's get married, I say frivolously and with the lightness I usually use when I talk about serious things. I'm only able to talk seriously and for hours about nonsense. For the important things, like love or death, or money, I always have to turn a phrase, raise an eyebrow and let out a nervous cackle, maybe out of modesty, or because I have a weak, lethargic character. Oscar is aware of it, and he's too clever to take a proposal like that seriously, which for one reason or another – love, jealousy, fear – we've had on the table for many years.

He hoots.

— Are you nuts? Where would we live? I don't fit in your house.

— Ah. I consider how the presence of a man might upset the status quo of the loft where I now live with the boys. It's like a cosy little burrow hanging between trees, smelling of currants and roses, butter biscuits, wood and pepper and moss. I could never leave my loft, my wooden, light-filled loft. It's something I love.

We're quiet for a minute.

— You see? You're incapable of making sacrifices for anyone.

— That's not true, I protest weakly.

— Incapable of renouncing anything from your disorderly, infantile life, always trying to be different, doing the opposite of what everyone else does.

— Not true. And what about you, so rigid and uncompromising? I saw the look on your face yesterday when the children were eating a third chocolate crêpe.

— Because it's completely idiotic. Three chocolate crêpes does not a dinner make. And I don't see why you have to eat out every night. It's like spending money just to spend it.

I remember the endless arguments over whether Nico really needed another pair of trainers, and my blatant profligacy with money – it was always my own money, never his – and how the children shouldn't leave the table until they'd eaten everything on their plates, and they shouldn't be allowed to watch more than an hour of television a day, or they shouldn't be permitted to sleep in our bed, or they shouldn't have too many toys. And the cleaning lady who didn't steal, but she was so incredibly lazy that he would pay her a few days late to show disapproval with her performance. And yes, the restaurant is charming but we could have eaten the same thing at home. And the day it snowed in Barcelona and we had to rescue the children from school, walking all the way across the city. I lived the experience as an adventure – the heroine whose boots were soaking wet battled the elements to save her young who couldn't get home with the babysitter because the subway stopped working and there wasn't a single taxi, amid a cottony and festive chaos where the cars' lights, like Christmas lights, illuminated the tiny snowflakes that stuck to my lips and eyelashes – and you thought the whole thing was just a huge nuisance. The scaffolding that structures Oscar's life – being reasonable, realistic and doing what's obligatory – are like prison bars to me. And my constant tidal waves are tantamount to all that's trivial, haughty and reckless in the world.

— All right, lovers it is, then.
— No. For me it's all or nothing.
— Wait a second. Let's talk this through.
— We've talked it through a thousand times, Blanquita. You don't want a relationship. He says it jadedly, quietly.

— At least not with me, he adds in the neutral tone that cuts to the quick, and in the same fell swoop takes off both our heads. — And anyway, I have to leave, I have a lot of work in Barcelona.

I know it's not true, it's Friday, it's summer, and that lately he spends the weekends with his girlfriend.

— You're going out with that bitch again, right? I don't want to feel sorrow; it's too fine an emotion, it's modulated and deep, and long-winded. I prefer to get angry.

— She's not a bitch. She's actually really nice, he says. I jump out of bed groaning.

— Oh, 'nice'. Well, isn't that just a stimulating virtue? I murmur. And slam the door behind me, turning a deaf ear to his joking pleas.

For the rest of the morning, Oscar cheerfully attends his mobile phone, sending and receiving text messages. He leaves after lunch.

— I'll always be here for you, he said on his way out — you'll never lose me.

— Really? I respond.

— Of course. Nobody will ever love you the way I do, he answers with a serious expression.

— Well, some day someone else might think the same thing.

Acting as if he hasn't heard me, he says: — Life goes around and comes around. Anything's possible.

— True.

Our relationship has probably taken all the turns allotted it in life, and the roulette wheel stopped this one last time on a losing number. We are completely penniless now. I'd love to rebuild the world, or an almost-world, with the pieces I have left, put the puzzle back together and bring things back to the way they used to be, not have to go outside again, but I guess there are just too many pieces missing now.

He tries to kiss me on the lips, but I turn my head.

Guillem shouts as soon as I close the door, happy to be the only adult male once again (Damián, being merely a guest and without a sentimental relationship with me, doesn't count).

— Thank God he's left – he's so stiff, I don't understand what you see in him.

I try to laugh. — Yeah, you're right – the other day he wanted to stop the boys eating three crêpes for dinner.

I give the children an outrageous amount of money to go out and buy some pancakes with Argentine caramel at a place near the church. I tell myself it doesn't really matter, that it's true about how life goes round and round. But I feel as though I've swallowed a piece of glass.

13

The boys, exhausted after spending another day on the boat, head straight for bed. It's almost pitch black on the terrace, and the town's warm, happy, summery sounds hover in the air. The church looks magnificent, illuminated like a theatre set, as if exacting revenge on the sea for taking centre stage by day. But the sea submits now, becoming a dusky, taciturn pond, reflecting the silvery moonlight and the street light's yellow shades. The houses spiral about the church's whitewashed wings, as if they were under its protection. Damián and I, like two sick children taking a dose of mother's cough syrup, smoke the joints that had been so industriously rolled by Elisa. I watch them whisper in each other's ear on the opposite side of the terrace. She collects herself, and talks without looking at him, while he listens to her and looks out over the horizon, smiling. Guillem and Sofía are drinking – I've never seen Guillem smoke dope, or Oscar either for that matter – and he's trying to talk her into helping him weed the back garden. Some of Damián's friends are here, people I've met on several occasions at dinners and social events. I watch them from a distance, through the cruel and petty lucidity that comes with alcohol and dope, and the black ideas provoked by Oscar, and now Santi, whom I've arranged to see tomorrow. The men are friendly enough, if a bit uptight, and use culture and a very calculated sense of humour as a way of protecting themselves from the world, and to compensate for being physically unattractive and uncomfortable in their own skins – which of course doesn't stop them from being crude and implacably harsh judges of feminine beauty. A sort of affected and condescending gallantry becomes a substitute for good manners. They're dressed very tidily, conventionally, as if their mothers still chose their wardrobe and ironed their clothes. Their weapons of choice are intelligence, sarcasm, and an infallible eye for detecting the defects in others. Two of them are writers. The girls are pretty and slim, clever, cautious and modest. They don't say much, existing sweetly and with suspicious affability, all the while sneaking glances to register what's around them. They've brought a guitar. Juanito, the shorter, funnier and more aloof of the bunch, starts playing and singing and the women join in. They render South American love songs with grace and enthusiasm. Maybe they're playing that song you liked so much at that snack bar on the beach, who knows? Sofía belts out the lyrics of the first ranchera she knows, and she and Guillem start dancing. Pedro, Damián's other friend, comes up to me as considerate and affectionate as ever. He talks about the last time he was in New York, his children from different mothers, scattered around the world, one here and the other in Amsterdam, and how much money they cost. We've had lunch together a few times and he always made a show of paying, maybe too much of a show.

— How are you holding up? he asks.

— Not well. Tired. I miss my mother. Maybe I should have lied, I think. Told him that everything is fine, all is under control. Truth is a door I open only once in a while; otherwise, I keep up the high, slippery wall of fibs and courtesy. The quick smile also protects me like a blanket, but today I have neither the strength nor the willpower to raise the wall. — Sometimes I feel as if I've lost everything, I add, expecting him to respond with the usual silence that meets all circumstances dealing with death. I take another hit of the joint. I look at Damián, who is also smoking slowly, like my reflection on the other side of the terrace. His eyes are bloodshot and yet twinkling, and they look into mine as if through a mirror darkened by smoke, as if we were trying to recognise each other. I smile; he must be a good drinking buddy, enthusiastic and fearless; I suspect Elisa – as well as sleeping with him, and acting like his mother – protects him from himself.

— Oh, come on, Blanca, you know perfectly well that's not true, Pedro interrupts me, breaking the drugged, sleepy and unanticipated link that was tying me to Damián. — You don't look like a person who's been left with nothing, he says brusquely, opening his eyes like a cunning monkey, as if suddenly he's aware that he's talking to someone a lot stupider than he thought.

— Nearly every person I've most loved in my life has died. I'm losing so many of the important places of my childhood and adolescence, I explain.

— But you observed these people and these places when they belonged to you, right? he continues with the slightly irritated tone of a professor before an unexpectedly disappointing pupil. I realise that both of us are completely stoned.

— Yes, of course. I could describe each and every corner of my mother's house. I know and remember the changing colours of the mahogany shelves where she kept her books, from mahogany to garnet and finally black according to the time of day and when dusk fell. I know the exact temperature of my father's hands, like bread fresh out of the oven, and in a snap I could draw you the half-empty glass of red wine he always kept in the kitchen. Want me to draw it for you? I could do it right now. Go on, get me a pencil and paper and I'll draw it for you.

— Sweetheart, he continues as he stands by my side, — love is not the only thing that makes things belong to us, it's also our power of observation; the cities we've visited, the adventures we've lived, the people, everything. Everything you've done or experienced without indifference, attentively, they belong to you. You can call them up whenever you want. His thin face, like Captain Haddock's butler, scrunches into an ugly grimace. I feel like smoothing it out softly with my fingertips, but instead I pass him the joint.

— No, dude, no. I've never called him 'dude' before. — I think there are certain things that we lose forever. In fact, I think we're more a sum of the things we've lost than of the things we've kept. I look up at the darkness of your bedroom, whose door Patum has been guarding since we arrived. I never went to the cemetery to see you today, in the end.

Slowly but surely, a thread weaves its way among those of us who are getting more and more stoned, like a delicate spider's web, unwittingly excluding those who remain sober. I smile at Damián from the fog and he seems so far away. I feel Elisa's immediate, inquisitorial glare, a person who barely drinks and doesn't even smoke cigarettes any more, full of a kind of relentless scrutiny for anyone except her boyfriends. It glides over me like something slightly oily and unpleasant, but I continue the mute, absurd conversation that my eyes are engaging in with her ever-fuzzier boyfriend. I make the sign for him to come over, afraid he might dissolve away entirely and disappear forever into the mist. He sits down beside me and chats with Pedro. For a second, it seems as if all is well, nothing is lost and Pedro is right. Music blends with my friends' voices and the rumour of the sea is like a familiar and protective nanny. I rest my head on Damián's shoulder and close my eyes.

I wake up with an epic hangover. It must be late because I don't hear the children, who must have left for the beach already, and because of the brazen, unforgiving light that's streaming through the window. Closing my eyes does nothing to stop it from perforating my eyelids and temples. I put on my Lady of the Camellias dressing gown and move as little as possible to keep my steps from reverberating in my head. I prepare a herbal tea and browse through an old newspaper. That's when Elisa shows up.

— Hey! I'm happy to see her – we haven't had a chance to talk much since she started going out with Damián.

— What a great time we had last night! Your friends are really nice, what a great idea to bring a guitar. We should do it again sometime.

She looks at me with a stern expression and doesn't say a word. Her face is tired; she has shadows under her eyes, but not the good kind, from having had a lot of fun and kisses, but the insomniac and troubled kind.

— Elisa, what's wrong?

— You know perfectly well what's wrong.

— No, I don't. My head's ready to burst with a migraine, so I'm not really in the mood for a guessing game. I begin to feel a little apprehensive, a vague disquiet regarding the mists of the previous evening.

— Last night I saw something that disturbed me and made me feel really sad. She pauses and looks at me with the same hard, sombre expression as, well, now that I think of it, as the night before.

— What did you see?

— I saw you say goodnight to Damián.

I burst out laughing, thinking she's pulling my leg.

— Yeah, he kissed me on the mouth, like he always does.

It's not the first time, and it won't be the last, that I say goodbye to a friend after a night of partying with a quick peck on the lips, I think. Yesterday evening, it was on his initiative and for a second I considered rejecting him, but I thought, amused, that he was just being a shameless scoundrel (in an age of cowards, the bold deserve recognition), and that's when Elisa's dark glance shot at me like a bolt of lightning. But everything happened so quickly, and by the time I was able to finish my thought, the flutter of his lips on mine had also finished.

— Oh, that was on his initiative . . . Thank goodness! And then Pedro kissed me too.

— Blanca, darling, I'm not talking about Pedro. I already know you're kissed by many.

I laugh again, unable to believe the conversation we're having, it's so unlike us, so far from our usual friendship.

— Elisa, you can't honestly think I'm trying to seduce your boyfriend. Are you nuts?

— Yes, maybe I am going absolutely bat crazy, but I know what I saw . . . though naturally, I could be wrong.

— Elisa, he didn't kiss me, our lips brushed each other. We were totally stoned. We're friends. But don't worry, I promise I'll never give him another kiss of any variety.

— Blanca, sweetie, I've been watching you for days, seen how you're constantly grabbing on to his arm.

I burst out laughing again.

— It's true, she says under her breath.

— I like Damián, I think he's a nice guy, but that's it, end of story. But really, there's no problem, I'll stop showing any physical signs of affection. Elisa! I stand up and grab her by the shoulders trying to wake her up from a bad dream. — You seriously think that I would fool around with Damián? It's absolutely ridiculous.

— Oh, sure! she cries, now even more resentful than before. It's so disgusting to think you'd want to screw Damián – I'm the only one stupid enough for that, right?

— No, that's not what I mean. I'm trying to say that I would never get involved with a friend's boyfriend. You must know that. With the number of men out there in the world . . . I begin to realise that it doesn't really matter what I say.

— No, you just throw yourself at them and say goodbye with kisses on the lips.

— I promise you that 'throwing myself' at a man is something entirely different. Elisa, we're just friends, there's nothing going on.

— Blanca, it's not friendship, it's flirting.

— Friendship is always flirtatious.

— Oh! In that case, just go right ahead! She makes a sweeping gesture with her hand, as if she were ordering the troops to advance.

— Elisa, seriously, I don't fancy Damián, I just think he's nice. And our lips barely touched. I also realise I'm going to have a migraine all day long. — Anyway, kissing on the lips isn't an intimate gesture – I kiss my boys on the mouth, my male friends and also my girlfriends.

— You want to know something, Blanca? This childish idea you have of a new kind of society that theoretically our generation is building while nobody's looking, where we all understand each other and kiss whomever we want whenever we want and go in and out of relationships like we go in and out of our houses and have children with this person and that person, it only works when you don't give a shit about other people.

— I don't give a shit about other people.

— You don't give a shit about anyone. Except for your children and maybe your mother. And you know what? I'm tired of psychoanalysing you. Your mother died, she was old and very sick, and she suffered a lot over the last six months and she screwed you over a lot, but she had a wonderful life, she loved and was loved, she was successful, she had friends, children, she had fun, and according to you, she always did whatever she damn well pleased. And you loved her and now you're sad and a little bit lost, but that doesn't give you the right to turn everyone else's lives upside down.

— I never wanted to turn anyone's life upside down. You know what your problem is, Elisa? And without giving her the chance to respond I say: — You're a coward, that's why you've always refused to try drugs, that's why you don't want to have children, that's why you always need a man by your side. Out of fear. Admit it, you live in a little cage. I'm convinced my left temple is going to explode at any moment, and a little piece of my brain is going to shoot out and finally settle the argument.

— So says the poor little rich girl who lives off a trust fund, who has never gone to a public hospital in her life and complains that we're 'slumming' if we arrange to meet in certain areas of the city, including, by the way, where I happen to live. Don't kid yourself – the person who lives in a cage is you, and your totally make-believe, fantasy world has about as much to do with reality as you.

— I don't live off a trust fund.

— I'm leaving. It's impossible to argue with someone who is constantly trying to be facetious. Damián is waiting for me in the car park.

As she's walking across the yard I yell out:

— And you know what? My kisses are mine. I don't have to explain them to anyone, I'll give them out as I see fit and to whomever I want. Like money. Except that everyone has kisses, they're much more democratic, and a lot more dangerous too, since they put us all on the same level. And if you did the same, if we all did the same, the world might be a little more chaotic but a lot more fun –

— Goodbye, Blanca.

She turns round and leaves. I hear someone whistle and when I look up I see Guillem leaning out the window. He stares at me with his jaw dropping, points his finger at his temple and makes the gesture to say 'you're both cuckoo'. I slam the door violently, and start bawling.

14

Guillem goes off to find the others at the beach so they can take the boat to the lighthouse, and I spend the rest of the morning like a lost soul, at home alone with Patum, holding a tiny pack of crushed ice to my forehead trying to appease the migraine. Patum already knows you aren't here, she won't go into your room, just sits by the door waiting for you, sniffing every corner of the house to find your smell, or some sign that you'll be coming back. Me too. I thought about going back to one of the places we visited together, to Athens, Venice, New York. Yesterday Guillem told me the vet had warned you that Patum doesn't have a lot of time left, that she might not even last through the winter. She's the last of the glorious litter of puppies that was born at home and who were adopted by your friends. I remember feeling so nervous and how excited you were watching Nana leave slick little packages of throbbing meat all around the house. I think there were nine in all; one died a few hours later, but the others survived. I made you build a huge wooden box that you put next to the bed, and we spent weeks watching over them and caring for them, completely indifferent to the breeder's smell that invaded your refined bedroom with its raspberry-coloured carpet, mirrors and mahogany chest of drawers, decorated with the paintings of voluptuous women. You took charge of everything, made sure the stronger ones let the weaker and thinner ones eat, and that Nana had a chance to rest. It wasn't difficult to recognise the girl you were; I loved her too, that girl.

Patum is looking at me with a pitiful expression; she loves me irrationally and disproportionately, perhaps the only kind of love that's worth having, the kind we don't deserve. But now she's Guillem's dog, maybe she always was – he gave her a name after all. Things, and maybe even people, belong to those who know how to give them their names. I'm afraid of her dying, and how this side of the divide is emptying out; there are days when I feel the dead breathing on my neck, like a silent and proud force pushing me forward, but there are other days when behind and before me are only cliffs. I think about Rey – he was left without an owner, too.

I wait for the children to get back from their boating trip, happy and exhausted, Edgar is getting browner and browner and Nico growing more and more freckly as the days go by. I can't help but cackle like the wicked witch of the fairy tale, thinking about the hearts that are going to be broken, and the girls that will inevitably break theirs, in the sentimental tragedies that await us. They're both so gifted – trusting, sensitive, passionate, modest – so fated for the game, even though they aren't aware of it yet. I excuse myself from lunch and go to my bedroom, waiting for sleep to come and the complete darkness that will alleviate my headache. I can hear them at the table amid laughter and shouts while Sofía comes to ask if I need anything and dabs my forehead with a little lemon-scented cologne. After a while, Guillem comes down.

— How is our Lady of the Camellias feeling? he asks, sitting down next to me on the bed. — Are you hungry? He's still in his swimming trunks, yellow and sky-blue shorts that reach halfway down his thigh, and one of his school T-shirts. He's tanned and seems to be in a good mood.

— No, no thanks.

— I don't understand why you smoke that shit.

— I don't either. Give me your hand, please. Keep me company for a while?

He grasps my hand with a growl; Guillem isn't given to verbal or physical gestures of affection, the type of paraphernalia that most of us dress our love in. And yet, he will always do what's right, decent and compassionate in any serious situation. The rest of the time, he picks on himself, on everyone else, he drinks and he tries to help his students learn something about history. I didn't realise it when I was with him, or when we separated, but now I know there's still time left for us.

— Your friend Sofía has a screw loose, he says nonchalantly but looking straight at me with a certain sense of urgency.

— Yeah, she's a real character.

— She really cares about you. Yesterday she spent hours talking about you.

— And I care a lot about her too, she's a great person. You like her, don't you?

— She's not bad, but if you would prefer . . . He leaves the sentence suspended in mid-air. I smile, thinking I'm on my deathbed and my ex-husband is asking my permission to go out with my best friend. Surely I'll ask for his blessing one of these days when I fall in love again, too. He and Oscar are the closest things I have to a father.

— Go right ahead, I say, squeezing his hand. — But if she hurts you in any way, I'll have to kill her.

He smiles. — Let's hope it won't be necessary, he says, considering the matter closed. — Well, I'm going up. If I'm not there the boys don't eat. And he leaves the room without making a sound.

Thank goodness jealousy has an expiry date, I think, as I soothe my right eye with the ice pack. Love never expires, though, at least not in my case. I still love all the people I have ever loved, and I can't help but see the person for what he or she was before everything turned to ash. I still see them untainted, despite all the desertions and disloyalties on my part or on theirs. I refuse to renounce a single one of my loves or my wounds over some stupid sense of heroics. It would be like denying my own self. I know that not everyone understands; the blanket of shame is heavy and resistant, and many people wear their hatred and resentment as badges, or like swords to brandish with as much pride and doggedness as the things that bear their affection. Guillem and I separated so many years ago! I love him, but I freed him of my love. A person can free themselves, of course, but it's always easier if the other person has the generosity of clearly giving you the boot since it's never easy to renounce another person's love; poor Oscar, on the other hand, still drags my shackles around – as I do his – like the ghost of Canterville, heavily, and making a huge racket.

I sleep through until late afternoon. When I finally wake up, I have a message from Damián apologising for getting me into this 'mess', and another from Santi suggesting we meet for a couple of hours at a hotel. I erase Damián's without responding and arrange to meet Santi later.

Before leaving, I see Guillem and Sofía tangled together in the hammock on the terrace. Úrsula is noisily washing the dishes, Edgar is in his room playing on the computer and the younger ones have been in bed for a while already. The crickets chirp as I cut across the garden. A small salamander is startled by my footsteps, and darts off quickly between the still warm stones. The streets are filled with people, contented families, young couples full of hope, slumbering children, open shops and crowded terraces looking out over the silent, dark-pewter sea. A local band is playing Cuban *pachanga* music in the town's square, trying to get the summer visitors to groove without much luck; a few stray parents, pushed forward by little children, venture some steps to the music's rhythm. I see the mysterious stranger when I pass by the casino, sitting at the door drinking beer with his friends. I also recognise the girl he was with at the funeral and she smiles at me. He gets up when he sees me and comes over.

— Hey. How's it going?

His nose is peeling and his big toe is sticking out of a hole in his grimy espadrilles. He looks at me attentively and a little stand-offishly, but I know the days spent in the sun, the golden reflection of the street lamps recently lit, the hours of sleep and the prospect of my running off to meet a lover are all playing in my favour, adding a bit of colour to my cheeks and a twinkle in my eye. I perk up and take out a cigarette. He too changes his posture to show off his plumage, plunging his hands into his pockets and imperceptibly cutting me off from the direction I was walking. He may be a little younger than me, I realise for the first time with a blend of irrelevance and apprehension. I never consciously used my youth as a weapon of seduction, but neither did it occur to me before now that it would come to an end. I'm suddenly struck with the notion, not inconsolably, that the onset of physical decline will eventually bring the mental kind along with it.

— Fine.

— Would you like a drink?

— I'd love one, but I'm in a bit of a rush.

— Yeah, so many men, so little time.

It makes me think about Santi, who must be waiting for me by now. The second we arranged to meet, I lost interest in actually seeing him. I think about the other men all of whom were merely patches to hide my deep reticence at building a new relationship only to have it end up in ruins anyway. Yet it's getting harder to ignore how perverse loneliness can be, and how easy it is to slide down the slippery slope of despair.

— Well, next time, he says and moves to the side. He kisses me goodbye, and I feel his blond, scratchy cheeks against mine, so warm and promising.

— Actually, I think I may still have a few minutes, I say looking at my wristwatch and pretending to calculate the time. — By the way, what's your name?

— Martí.

— Nice to meet you. My name's Blanca. I stretch my hand out automatically, a little absurd and ceremonious since I already know from the look in his eye and the touch of his cheek that he'll shake it firmly and that his palm will be warm and dry.

We join the group of friends, another man and two women, who all greet me amiably and with the wry, affable curiosity typical of people from the Emporan. The women are single, free of the commitments that can be counted in years or children, that might make them watch what they say or else loosen their tongues – I've never heard anyone talk about men more crudely or cruelly than women who are supposedly happily married. They poke fun at the guys. The men listen good-humouredly, slightly sarcastic in their repartee, but without resorting to the annoying stereotypes we sometimes attribute to one another, that are usually false and, what's worse, boring.

— What do you look for in a man? the woman I've never seen before asks me suddenly, with the type of familiarity these sorts of conversation often breed in women. She's young, with chestnut hair, dark eyes and a hungry gaze.

I think for a minute, not knowing whether to answer seriously or with a joke, deliciously conscious of Martí's straight-backed, gentle presence by my side.

— I like men who make me want to be cleverer than I am, and I add in a whisper: — since usually they want me to be sillier and more stupid.

— Oh, baby girl! the woman says, laughing. — You're asking for way too much.

The conversation about what men and women look for in the opposite sex continues, though Martí and I hardly participate.

We split from the group almost naturally, and without any conscious effort on either one of our parts. I realise I'm a little nervous; I haven't said his name yet and the glass I was holding so firmly just a few minutes ago, surrounded by people and laughter, now seems to be trembling. I also feel terribly bad for making Santi wait at the hotel.

— I really do have to get going now. It's late. And as a delaying tactic for the moment when I'll truly have to leave, I ask: — When's your birthday?

He looks at me with a puzzled expression.

— Don't tell me you believe in horoscopes.

— No, not really. I just wanted to know so I can give you a new pair of espadrilles.

He looks at his feet and wiggles his big toe.

— But these are perfect, he says, blushing a little. — They're air-conditioned.

— Oh? Let me give them a try. Suddenly I'm back in the game, where I feel more comfortable and sure of myself, a much less trivial place than people give it credit for; the most dazzling certainties of my life have come precisely while I was messing around. He removes an espadrille hesitatingly, and places it in front of me. I submerge my foot in the huge shoe, nearly the size of a small life raft, and feel the straw sole hard and dry under-neath, and the stiff, sea-salt stained navy canvas rubbing against my instep. — A perfect fit, I say wiggling the red nail of my big toe, which looks as out of place there as a clown's nose in the middle of a washed face. — I think I'll keep them.

— Isn't that how Cinderella ends? She finds a shoe just her size? Martí says, looking at me with a calm smile.

— Oh, you're right. It hadn't occurred to me! I say,

removing my foot from the espadrille and giving it back.
— I have to get going. See you around, Martí. I kiss him
at the edge of his lips and run away, before my princess's
garb turns into rags and me into a pumpkin.

I've never been in a hotel in Cadaqués before, and though
the sight from the balcony is such a familiar one, I feel
like I'm back in that unsettling and foreign space of a
hotel room that's not meant for sleeping. It's a place
where you're always alone even when accompanied, like
a soldier preparing himself for battle; there's only a war-
rior's respite; short, deep and provisional.
— I'm so sorry – I know I'm late.
— Don't worry, but I'm nearly out of time.
Through the window I can see night has fallen
completely, it must be nearly midnight. I smile at his sad
face, the glassy eyes of a lost, addicted boy. He's never
angry; no matter what I do, no matter what I say, Santi
never gets angry with me. I think he considers my rude-
ness and outbursts the price to pay for an unequal relationship, because he doesn't realise that you can't take
something away that hasn't ever been given, and if we
split up, I'm the one with the least to lose.
He undresses me methodically and with a sort of slow,
grateful clumsiness. His eyes are red and his mouth tastes
like paper towels – he must have smoked a joint while he
was waiting for me. I let him go about things, sensitive
and alert, anxious for the moment when I'll lose my

balance, and the warmth of my belly will spread like an explosion all over my body. He comes in a minute and a half, like a soft, docile baby, incapable of taking me with him to the other side, and then spends the following ten apologising, instead of putting them to better use.

— I'm really sorry, I'm just mega-tired.

— Don't worry about it, I lie, in a bad mood now, as my heated body cools off, my lips dry out and my desire flutters about the room, without a specific objective, like a listless, but persistent cloud.

He gets up suddenly and I watch his reflection in the wardrobe mirror. For the first time I realise how small his head is and that he's going bald.

— You use 'mega' too often. I say, slowly sharpening my words.

— You used to love it – it used to make you die laughing.

— My mother would roll over in her tomb if she heard you.

He smiles sweetly with his nicotine-stained teeth. I look at him carefully and he seems like a costume that slowly begins to disintegrate – the brown skin, the four-day beard, the dry martinis, the ferocious wolf hands, the bracelet from some music festival past. It's not that the man standing before me is ugly – on the contrary – but he's not the man I fell in love with, he's no longer a whole, he's just a set of qualities and defects, a man like any other, for whom my love is no longer a charm against being out in the cold.

— That's too bad. I have to get going, he says with orphan eyes, while the invisible cloud that's hanging above his reckless head swells with the coming rain.

— You know what's going to happen, don't you?

— What?

— Your wife is going to leave you again, and she's going to fall in love with another man.

— It won't be easy for her to find someone else – she's not like you.

I recall the arrogant woman in the turquoise dress in the butcher's shop with a bit of compassion, and think how sometimes we say miserable and vile things about the people we love the most.

— And then I won't love you any more.

He remains pensive, seemingly more concerned over the possibility that his wife could find another man than that some day I won't feel like running into his arms, as if it were something that hadn't crossed his mind, as if what had happened once was a sort of natural disaster that could never happen again. He dresses in silence.

— I haven't fucked my wife in a long time. He drops it like a filthy gift at my feet, like a dog who leaves a rodent's rotting corpse as a trophy after a walk in the woods.

— I don't care, that's none of my business, I say, feeling disgusted. He's never mentioned intimacy with his wife before. And I add: — I think we should stop seeing each other.

— Shit, shit, shit, he yells and clutches his head with both hands like an actor trying to convey dismay. — I know I don't give you a lot, but I can't stop seeing you. And he whispers, as if he's afraid to say it, as if it were a lie: — I love you so much.

That's been our problem, I think, surprised to see that I've begun thinking in the past tense, that instead of loving me, you have loved me so much. But I don't say anything because it's already too late and because there's no conversation in the world as pathetic and more destined for failure as two people trying to gauge their love.

His mobile phone rings; his wife has just got back from a concert in the next town and wants to know where he is. He looks at his very expensive wristwatch, a gift from his father-in-law, which he wears as if it were a wedding ring, and then looks at me with glassy eyes.

— I have to go.

— Yeah, me too.

— We'll see each other soon, OK? He smashes his lips clumsily against mine, which remain passive.

As he walks away, I notice how crooked his legs are.

I sit down to smoke in the town square. The band is still playing but the audience has changed; the creatures of the night have replaced the families, greater in number and more interested in dancing. Until you became ill and died, it had never occurred to me to sit down on a bench in the street. If I was in the street it was to go somewhere or to take a walk, but now I enjoy this stillness in the midst of people, these small rafts of public safety. The world can be divided into those who sit on the benches in the street and those who don't. I guess I now form a part of the collective of old folks, immigrants and loiterers, those who don't know where else to go. Then I catch a very tall, hunched, vaguely familiar figure in the multitude, his skinny arms that seem to go on forever, raised high above people's heads. He's either dancing or waving to me.

— Blanca! Darling!

He kisses me on the lips, like he did the first day, a thousand years ago, five minutes after we met, in the middle of a tableful of people. I think fleetingly of Elisa, with her sharp, shrewd rat's face, armed with all manner of Freudian theories on how to confront and tame the world; too bad she isn't here, she would be able to explain everything to me, and we'd laugh and surely she'd say it was all your fault.

— Nacho!

— What are you doing here by yourself?

— I don't know. Lately everyone's been abandoning me, my ex-husband, my best friend, my lover –

— Come on, he says, grabbing my hand, — let's find a party.

I glance at him as we walk along the town's streets. The king of the world, the junkie athlete, the unrepentant womaniser, has turned into a beggar covered in ashes. We've known each other since we were children but we didn't become friends until I turned twenty, when the age difference – he's nine years older than me – stopped being so apparent and didn't matter any more. I stopped being a little puppy to him, though he still called me one, and he stopped being an old man to me. He had the perfect combination of lightness and darkness, the kind only star-crossed, romantic men have, that electric luminosity that draws others to them like moths to a flame, with his big doe eyes, and debauched, drug-infused, lifestyle – idle, chaotic and self-absorbed. His physical beauty was so remarkable for so many years that no woman could resist him; I couldn't either, and we watched the sun come up more than once, huddled together on some beach or under some arch. But despite the affection we claimed, we never went out of our way to see each other in Barcelona, where we both live – we never even exchanged phone numbers. Nacho belongs to the summer just like the boating trips do, or the naps in the hammock, or the freshly baked bread we buy straight from the oven on our way home after being out all night, kneaded by the arms of drowsy men who watch us devour it with sad eyes. He couldn't ever exist anywhere outside of Cadaqués. Cocaine became his only lover in the end; it transformed that ravishing smile into a tense and contorted rictus, stole his puppy eyes and exchanged them for shrewd, hungry and cloudy ones. His flexible, elegant body became nothing more than a skeleton. I think all of this as we walk up the cobblestone steps; he moves stiffly and it seems as though each stride causes pain, as if he were empty. I suppose every body tells its own story of voluptuousness, of horror and helplessness.

We come to a large house with white salons, old leather couches full of cushions and oriental rugs strewn across a red terrazzo floor. There are candles lit everywhere, some already completely consumed. The great French windows overlooking the town and the sea are thrown wide open, and the pale gossamer curtains flap like captive sails. There are a ton of people, music and drugs strewn across low tables, along with all manner of alcohol and the remains of fruit swooning in huge, colourful bowls. I recognise some of the town's other castaways, children of the first settlers, intellectuals and artists who arrived in Cadaqués during the sixties and filled it with beautiful, talented people who wanted to change the world but, above all, enjoy themselves. I recognise the children of that generation immediately, the wild ones, like me, were educated by lucid, brilliant, successful and very busy parents, adults who engaged the world as if it were a party, their party. We are, I think, the last generation who struggled for our parents' attention, which usually only came when it was already too late. Children weren't considered marvellous creatures, they were more like a big nuisance, little things that were only halfway formed. And they turned us into a lost generation of born seducers. We had to invent more interesting and sophisticated ways to attract their attention than pulling at their sleeve or bursting into tears. They demanded the same from us as they did from other adults, or at least that we didn't bother them. The first thing I ever showed you was a piece I wrote and which had won a prize in school – I must have been eight years old – and you told me not to show it to you again until I had written at least a thousand pages, that anything less wasn't a serious effort. Good grades were a given, bad ones an annoyance, borne without colossal rebukes or any form of punishment. My house is covered in my younger son's drawings and I listen to the older one play the piano with the same reverence as if he were Bach come back from the grave. Sometimes I ask myself what's going to happen when this new generation of children grow up, whose mothers consider maternity a new religion – women who breastfeed their children until they're five years old and alternate their tits with spaghetti, women whose only interest and preoccupation and reason for being are their children, who educate them as if they were going to rule an empire, who inundate social media with photos of their offspring, not only at their birthday parties or on trips, but also in the bathroom or at the urinal (there is no more shameless love than the contemporary maternal variety). They'll turn into such deficient human beings, as contradictory and unhappy as we are, maybe even more so? I don't think anyone can come out of being photographed while shitting unscathed.

We sit down on a couch with a couple of Nacho's friends. Immediately, they pass round the cocaine. Nacho accepts enthusiastically and starts to jump all around us playing air guitar to the music that's piping over the speakers, opening his legs wide and strumming the instrument. The girl offers me a line, but I refuse it.

— No thanks, I'm tired. And if I'm not in good shape tomorrow, my children are going to be angry.

— Oh, she says, looking at me surprised. — You have kids. Well, a line will get you going; it'll take the tired away. She's blonde and sweet and very thin and brown-skinned, her old T-shirt is a faded rose colour, her Indian trousers are nearly transparent and she's not wearing knickers.

— No, really, I'm fine thanks.

— Are you stupid or what? her boyfriend screams at her suddenly. — Didn't you hear her say no? Leave her alone.

And they shout at each other, although luckily the music is up so high their voices are drowned out, and all I can see are their frantic gestures. Nacho comes and goes bouncing around, and finally, after a few gin and tonics, I allow myself to be carried off to dance with him, like when we were young and still thought the world was going to fulfil all its promises and nothing mattered because everything would turn out just fine. When the song ends, we lie down on the couch together. That's when the sweet, blonde-haired girl comes running towards us.

— I was looking for you! Check it out, she says, showing

me a photo on her mobile phone, — they're my frozen eggs.

— Oh. I look at the unrecognisable image with a grey background and a few stains in a darker shade of grey without knowing what I'm supposed to say, while she looks at me expectantly. — They're very beautiful, I finally answer.

— Oh, aren't they though? she exclaims. They're for when I want to have kids some day. And she adds: — When I'm ready for them.

— How nice. I'm happy for you, I say.

— I just wanted to show them to you. Her eyes are a transparent blue and very candid, and they make my soul shiver, as if I could hover above them and see straight into her body the movement of little rivers of blood, and her heart that's at once skittish and brave.

After she leaves, Nacho says: — She's beyond the point of salvation. He might be salvageable, but she's too far gone. Her father is a very important doctor in Madrid and it was his idea to freeze her eggs.

He brushes my hair from my neck and starts kissing it, pecking at it like a bird.

— And what about us? he asks. — Are we going to sleep together? Like in the good old days?

I start laughing. — How old we've become! Imagine us twenty years from now. We're just getting started on our new old age, but it's still a joke, a distant shadow.

— Meaning we're not going to sleep together.

He bites my neck softly.

— I think what I really need is a friend.

— You already know how dreadful I am at that.

We both laugh.

— Yeah, well. I'm not particularly good at it either. But we stay cuddling each other for a while . . . I feel that cloudy and somewhat painful kind of exhaustion from the day convalescing in bed, the vague and persistent sorrow that permeates everything since you died, that I try to shuffle off but whose particles always come back to fall in exactly the same spot.

Nacho hugs me tightly, like a little boy holding a stuffed toy, but I feel his body still tense and anxious. I know he won't go to sleep as long as there is a speck of poison left in the house.

— It's time to go. It's very late, I say, freeing him.

He accompanies me to the door and takes my face into his hands and kisses me like he did a thousand years ago, when we were other people, his Don Quixote silhouette cut out against the threshold.

— Take care of yourself, little one. It's cold out there.

It's cooled down and there is a light grey, milky haze blurring the contours of things, which is going to turn pink and then orange shortly. Dawn is set to break soon – I must have been at the party for three or four hours. The music trails me a while until all I hear are my own footsteps falling on the grey slate, and the chatter of night birds. I don't want to go to sleep yet, I think I'll head down to the beach and watch the sunrise alone for once. Though like so many other things, maybe sunrises only acquire their true sense of triumph and redemption while in silent company. Instead of heading towards the sea, though, I begin walking up the mountain, following a maze of narrow, pebbled alleys that seem like passageways, and the line of walls built from stacked stones, magnificent ancient puzzles that never collapse, marking the edge of vegetable gardens and olive fields, where cats doze and watch over the town by day. I come across a child's shoe left atop one of the walls. My boys will be waking up in a little while, they're my own private spectacle of dreams and dawns, Edgar silent and meditative, who drags along with him the vestiges of night long into the day, like me, and Nico, who rushes straight into the new day decisively, gushing and cheerful. My legs feel heavy like they do in some of my nightmares but I don't stop. I drink in the day's new, unspoiled air and tell myself that tomorrow I'll stop smoking, as I slowly continue climbing the hill to the dirt esplanade with its two rickety trees, that serves as the campground car park. I used to come here often when I was young; I had an Italian friend who used to make me spaghetti with tomato sauce there, on an outdoor stove. I've forgotten his name, as I have the majority of the main characters of those bright and blissful summers when we soared above the town and the world, young people overflowing with euphoria and arrogance, so full of passion, so carefree. An old man crosses the campground carrying a pail in his hand, and nods to me before disappearing into the small pavilion where the showers are. I must be a sorry sight right now; if the bar were open I would have a coffee and wash my face, but it's still too early, the grey building is closed and dark. I continue walking until I catch sight of the hermitage, whose white-washed walls are blanching, and there stand the two black cypress trees like solemn and benevolent guardians at either side of the cemetery. And here I am, I made it to the end of the yellow brick road. Despite the fatigue, my heart is beating hard, my hands are freezing and they begin to tremble. There was a crowd of people last time I was here, and the living outnumbered the dead, we were in the majority, and my friends were with me. I fantasised about what it would be like to come here on my own. I imagined myself walking up the hill, serene and philosophical, already healed, maybe holding some wild flower in my hand that I had picked along the path. I look at the huge door, its dark, knotted wood, and stroke the heavy metal handle. I'm frightened, I'm weary, maybe it would be better to head home, get some sleep, take a rest, and come back at noon with someone else, or maybe not come back at all, maybe I'll never come back, it's a possibility. I push the door. It's closed. But cemeteries aren't supposed to close at night, I've seen a thousand horror films set in cemeteries at night. Surely it's just me being clumsy, the door can't possibly be locked. I push with my body against the door again, and work the heavy iron handle to no avail. I can't catch my breath and suddenly I realise I'm crying. I'll fix it, I'll fix it, there's a solution to every problem. I'll call the mayor and ask him to come and open the door for me. I'll climb the wall like Spider-Man. I'll write a letter to the newspaper full of spit and vinegar. I'll talk to Amnesty International. It can't be possible that the door won't open and that I can't get in. I take a deep breath. I'll do things the right way, without losing my temper, I'm sure everything will work itself out. I call at the door under my breath, 'Mum, Mum,' quietly, and holding my ear up against the heavy wood. I think I hear something shuffling, like the sound of cat's paws in the distance, but nobody comes to help me. I wriggle the heavy iron handle again and start banging on the door with all my strength, as if I were the one locked inside trying to get out, until the pain in my fists and the palms of my hands obliges me to stop. Feeling defeated and exhausted, I sit down on the bench at the hermitage's door. The sun had come up without my noticing it. A clear, rosy light caresses the silver olive trees, turns the white walls to red and the dew moistens the dirt roads imperceptibly. I'm as familiar with this particular light as if it were the call of a friend. I climb up onto the bench and peer over the wall, and catch sight of the field of olive trees and Port Lligat in the background, the small port where we used to keep the boat. That's when I see her. Walking along the pier with her faded blue-checked shirt on top of her swimsuit, the beautiful brown legs that were always full of bruises, walking pigeon-toed with little girl's sandals, glasses askew, a messy shock of hair sticking out from under a hat that's dried out from the salt water, accompanied by her three dogs – Patum, Nana and Luna, who are coming from a swim and joyfully on their way out to the boat. The surface of the sea is as still as a plate; the weather is glorious. Before going aboard, she turns round and smiles at me, saying:

— This too shall pass.

And winks.

EPILOGUE

You spent your last night alone. I'd been with you the whole day at the hospital holding your hand, and when the doctor told me you were doing better, I decided to go home for a little while. Even though I could tell just by looking at you that it wasn't true. I would have liked to die along with you, in the same room, at the same instant, and not the next morning when you were already dead. I wish I had been there for our last breath, holding your hand. Though I'm walking in the land of the living, more or less joyfully, more or less alone, there's a part of me that will always remain wherever you are. I still occasionally tell myself the story you told me once, when you were sitting on my bed and consoling me after my father died: Once upon a time, in a land far, far away, maybe in China, there was a very powerful emperor who was intelligent and compassionate, and who gathered all the wise men of his kingdom together, the philosophers, the mathematicians, the scientists, the poets, and said to them: 'I want a short sentence, that serves all possible circumstances, always.' So the wise men retired and spent months and months in contemplation. 'We have the phrase, sire, and it's the following: "This too shall pass."' And you added: 'Pain and sorrow pass, but so do joy and happiness.' Now I know it's not true. I'll live without you until I die. You taught me that the only form of infatuation is the kind that strikes the heart with the flash of an arrow (you were right), the love of art, of books, museums, the ballet, absolute generosity with money, grand gestures at the appropriate time, precision in actions and in words. Never to feel guilt, and to enjoy freedom, with all the responsibility that entails. At home, nobody ever knew how to deal with guilt; if we made a mistake, feeling guilty was never a form of redemption – we had to deal with the repercussions and move on. I don't think I ever heard you say, 'I'm sorry.' You gave me the gift of this outrageous laugh, the thrill of being alive, the ability to surrender to things completely, the love of games, contempt for everything you thought made life smaller and more constraining: pettiness, disloyalty, envy, fear, stupidity, and cruelty more than anything else. And a sense of fairness. Nonconformity. The dazzling awareness of joy at the moment you have it in your hand, before it flies away. I remember times when we'd catch each other's eye for a second, over a tableful of people, or strolling through some unknown city, or out at sea, and feel as if a little pixie dust was falling over our heads and that maybe we'd never be able to take to flight, as Peter Pan believed, but almost. And you'd flash me a smile from the distance and I knew that you knew that we both knew, and that we both secretly thanked the gods for that silly gift, that perfect swim in the high seas, that pink twilight, that side-splitting laughter after a bottle of grappa, the clownish things we did so that people who already loved us might love us just a little bit more. And your magnanimity; your knack for giving a name to things, for seeing them truly, your genuine tolerance with the faults and defects of other human beings. I doubt I've inherited your tolerance, but I know it when I see it, I can recognise it, and ever since you've gone, I try to find it in a hungry dog or the haggard eyes of a junkie going through withdrawal, I can smell it, I hear it, I can distinguish it (sometimes the gesture of a hand is enough), it's budding in my children, their courtesy and good manners, the complete lack of snobbery. Every person who comes home, and that includes some very strange people, very wounded, very foolish, are received by your grandsons kindly, with curiosity and respect, cautiously and affectionately. And whenever we drive by your last apartment, on Muntaner Street, I catch sight of your elder grandson through the rear-view mirror looking up at your balcony in silence. And I think maybe I should tell him that you're in a better place now, but I know it's not true, because there was nothing you liked more than being with your grandsons and me. The day will come when we talk all about you. I'm beginning to breathe a little better now and the nightmares have almost subsided. Some days I almost feel a little pixie dust fall on my head, not a lot and not very often, but it's a start. And now we have a new guest at home – his name is Rey. I'm trying to teach the children to take him out for a walk every day. The day before yesterday I took your jacket to the cleaner's; it'll be ready on Thursday, 'like new', they said.